'What do y...
playing at?'...
brilliant viole...
a marriage o...
don't you forget it.'

'A convenient marriage, yes, but also a legal
marriage—and as such you must know it is
usual to consummate the union.' His dark,
cynical gaze held hers, and she stared back
in appalled amazement. 'If anyone is playing
around here it is you.'

'Me? Are you out of your mind?'

'Who do you think you are kidding? I am no
fool. Your earthy little moans, the soft flush
of arousal colouring your skin are a complete
giveaway,' he declared throatily, and reached
out to brush a strand of hair over her shoulder,
not the least fazed by her angry outburst. 'You
want this just as much I do.'

THE GREEK TYCOONS

They're the men who have everything—
except brides…

Wealth, power, charm—
what else could a heart-stoppingly handsome tycoon
need? In the GREEK TYCOONS mini-series you have
already been introduced to some gorgeous
Greek multimillionaires who are in need of wives.

Now it's the turn of favourite Modern Romance™
author Jacqueline Baird, with her
attention-grabbing romance
Aristides' Convenient Wife!

ARISTIDES' CONVENIENT WIFE

BY
JACQUELINE BAIRD

MILLS & BOON®

First published in Great Britain 2007
Harlequin Mills & Boon Limited,
Eton House, 18-24 Paradise Road, Richmond, Surrey TW9 1SR

© Jacqueline Baird 2007

ISBN-13: 978 0 263 85318 6
ISBN-10:   0 263 85318 7

Set in Times Roman 10½ on 12¼ pt
01-0507-56227

Printed and bound in Spain
by Litografia Rosés, S.A., Barcelona

ARISTIDES' CONVENIENT WIFE

CHAPTER ONE

ENGLAND IN FEBRUARY was not a place he would have chosen
to be, Leon Aristides thought angrily as the freezing rain continued to lash down almost obscuring his view of the road. But
the letter he had received at his office in Athens yesterday
morning from a Mr Smyth, a partner in a firm of London so-
licitors, and the information enclosed within had totally
stunned him.

Apparently the man had read an article in the *Financial
Times,* mentioning the dip in the price of Aristides
International shares, where Leonidas Aristides had explained
it was an understandable market reaction to the tragic accident
that had claimed the lives of his sister and his father, the
chairman of the company, but the price would quickly recover.
The said Mr Smyth had informed him Delia Aristides was a
client of his and he wanted confirmation of her death as his
firm held a will made by the lady and he was the executor.

Leon's first thought was that it must be a hoax resulting
from the mention of his name in the paper, an unusual enough
circumstance in itself. The Aristides name occasionally
appeared in financial journals, but rarely if ever in the popular
press. A banking family, they belonged to the type of wealthy
élite that did not court publicity or fame but concentrated on

the fortune. Their privacy was so closely guarded that the general public barely knew they existed. But after a telephone call to Mr Smyth, Leon had quickly realised the man was serious and if he didn't act fast that anonymity might disappear all too soon. He had arranged to call him back later. Then he had finally taken the time to go through his sister's safety deposit box, something he should have done weeks ago, but which the constant pressures of business had prevented.

There were the jewels their mother had left her, as he had expected. But there was also a copy of a will drawn up two years ago by the same Mr Smyth of London and officially signed and witnessed. A will moreover that took precedence over the will held by the family lawyer in Athens that Delia had made at the age of eighteen at their father's instigation.

The information the new will contained so outraged Leon his initial reaction had been to tear the document into a million pieces. But only for an instant before his iron-cool control had reasserted itself and he had called one of his lawyers. The resultant conversation had made him think long and hard.

A return call to Mr Smyth and he'd had an early appointment with the man for the following day. At the crack of dawn this morning he had boarded his private jet heading for London. A sombre interview with the lawyer had confirmed the shocking news.

Apparently on Leon's verbal confirmation of Delia's death he had immediately drafted a letter to one Miss Heywood as instructed, informing her that Delia had died and she was a beneficiary of her will. Leon could do nothing about it now, but he had obtained the man's promise of absolute discretion in the matter and they had parted with a handshake. Mr Smyth was an honest man but no fool, a banking company like Aristides International was not one to upset unnecessarily.

Leon manoeuvred the rental car into the short drive. In the

ordinary course of events he usually travelled by a chauffeured limousine, but in this case absolute secrecy was required until he had assessed the situation. He stopped the car and glanced up at the house. Nestling in the Cotswold hills, it was a double fronted detached stone built house, surprisingly set in the corner of the walled grounds of a luxury hotel.

Which was why he had driven past the entrance drive to the Fox Tower Hotel and around the whole damn estate three times without connecting the entrance to the hotel with the home of Miss Heywood: The Farrow House, Foxcovet Lane. So much for satellite navigation systems. Finally, in frustration he had entered the hotel and booked a room for the night; it looked as if he was going to need one if he did not find the elusive Miss Heywood soon. Then with a few casual questions he had discovered where the house was and why it had taken him so damn long to find it.

A light shone from a downstairs window, hardly surprising given the gloominess of the day, and hopefully an indication Helen Heywood was at home. He had considered ringing her, but he did not want to warn her. The element of surprise was the best weapon in any battle, and this was a conflict he was determined to win.

A predatory gleam lightened his dark eyes as he opened the car door and stepped out onto the gravelled drive slamming the door behind him. Unless she had already received the letter from Mr Smyth, which was highly unlikely if the British postal service was anything like the Greek, the lady was in for one hell of a shock. Squaring his broad shoulders, he approached the front door with decisive steps and rang the bell.

No signal again. Helen slowly replaced the telephone on the hall table, a frown pleating her smooth brow. Her best friend

Delia Aristides led a hectic lifestyle but she usually called every week and visited at least once a month. Admittedly since Delia had returned to Greece last July she had occasionally missed a week or two, but now it was over six weeks without a call. What made it worse was Delia had promised her son, Nicholas, she would definitely visit in the New Year after cancelling her last three visits, but once again she had cancelled at the last minute. Helen had heard nothing since.

She chewed worriedly on her bottom lip. It wasn't fair to Nicholas, or to her for that matter. Nicholas had been at nursery school all morning and, after she had collected him and made his lunch, he was now taking his afternoon nap. She knew he would be awake in an hour, if not sooner, and she wanted to get in touch with Delia before that. But she only had Delia's cell phone number. Helen knew the address of the Aristides island home but not the telephone number, she had tried to get the number from enquiries but of course it had turned out to be ex-directory. She was at a loss as to what to do next.

Helen grimaced and picked up the post she had not yet had time to look at from the hall table. Maybe Delia had written, but it was a forlorn hope. Her friend had never written a letter in all the time she had known her, the nearest she got was a card at Christmas and birthdays. Telephone or e-mail were her preferred forms of communication.

The doorbell rang, and she dropped the post and, heaving a sigh, wondered who could be calling in the middle of the afternoon.

'All right, all right I'm coming,' she muttered as the bell pealed out again and continued to ring. Whoever it was they obviously were not big in the patience department, she thought as she walked down the hall to open the door.

Leon Aristides. Helen stiffened, her hand tightening on the door handle, unable to believe her eyes. For a fleeting moment she wondered if she had forgotten to wear her contact lenses and he was a figment of her imagination, but only for a moment.

'Hello, *Helen,*' a deep-throated voice drawled, and although she was slightly myopic there was nothing wrong with her hearing. Oh, my God, Delia's brother! Here, at her door.

'Good afternoon, Mr Aristides.' She automatically made the polite response, her shocked gaze flicking up over him. Six feet plus and immaculately clad in a dark business suit, white shirt and silk tie, he hadn't changed much in the years since she had last met him. He was just as big, and dark, and forbidding as she remembered.

With heavy-lidded dark eyes and angular cheekbones, a large straight nose and a wide mouth, he looked hard rather than handsome. But he was physically attractive in a raw, masculine way. Unfortunately for Helen, he still had the same disturbing effect on her as he had the first time they had met, bringing a sudden fluttering in her stomach that she determinedly put down to nerves. She couldn't possibly still be afraid of the man. She was twenty-six, not seventeen any more.

'This is a surprise. What are you doing here?' she finally asked, eyeing him warily.

She had met him nine years ago, the one time she had gone on vacation with Delia to her family holiday home in Greece, and she had been left with a lasting impression of cynical arrogance and powerful masculinity.

She had been walking along the beach when a deep voice had called out demanding to know who she was. She had understood that much Greek. Glancing towards the sea, she had seen a man standing on the shoreline. She had known it was a private beach, but as Delia's guest she had had every right to be there, and in her innocence she had called out a response and walked towards him, concentrating on trying to bring him into focus. As her vision had improved she had offered her name with a smile, and held out her hand, then stopped and stared, her hand suspended in mid-air.

He had been tall and broad with a white towel draped around his lean hips, and the musculature of his magnificent bronzed body had been so clearly defined Michelangelo himself could not have sculpted better.

His gaze had captured hers, and the breath had stopped in her throat. There had been something dark and dangerous swirling in the black depths of his eyes that had made her heart beat faster. Every primitive sense she had possessed had told her to run but she had been paralysed by the physical presence of the man. Then he had finally spoken, and his sarcastic comment rang in her head to this day.

'Flattered though I am, and available as you so obviously are, I am a married man. You should try asking before ogling.' And he had walked away. She had never been so embarrassed before, or since.

'I would have thought that was self-evident.' The sound of his voice jerked her back to the present. 'I am here to see you. We need to talk.' He smiled but she noticed the smile didn't touch his eyes.

Helen didn't want to talk to him. She shuddered at the thought.

After their first meeting, for the rest of her stay in Greece she had tried to avoid him. It had not been too hard. With the constant flow of sophisticated friends and family to the Aristides home, it had been quite easy for two young girls to go unnoticed. On the rare occasion when Helen had had no option but to be in his company she had addressed him with cool politeness. When his beautiful wife Tina had arrived near the end of Helen's stay, she had only been able to wonder what the happy-go-lucky American woman saw in such an aloof, cynical man.

For Helen his scornful and deeply embarrassing comment to her, coupled with the senior Mr Aristides' distant politeness to both her and his daughter, simply confirmed what Delia had told her when they had first become friends at school.

According to Delia the reason she was at boarding-school in England rather than at home in Greece was because her father and her brother had agreed she needed to improve her English, but the reality was they had both decided she needed the discipline of a girls-only boarding-school. Apparently she had been caught smoking and flirting with a fisherman's son. No big deal according to Delia, who had personally thought it had more to do with the fact that her mother had committed suicide when she was twenty months old, from depression after her birth. Her father had blamed her for the death of his wife, and preferred her out of his sight.

To quote Delia, her father and brother were both stiff-necked chauvinist pigs. Ultra-conservative wealthy bankers totally devoted to the family business of making money, the females in their lives chosen simply as assets to enhance the business.

Delia had had no intention of being married for the benefit of the family company, as her mother and sister-in-law had been. She had been determined to stay single until she was at least twenty-five and then her father could not prevent her from inheriting the banking shares her mother had left in trust for her. Helen over the years had helped her to do just that.

Recalling Delia's low opinion of her brother, Helen stared at the tall, wide-shouldered man in front of her. His black hair was plastered to his head by the driving rain, but he still exuded the same shattering aura of aggressive male power that had so frightened her the first time they had met.

'Are you going to ask me in?' His dark eyes narrowed on her face. 'Or is it your habit to keep visitors wet and freezing on the doorstep?' he mocked.

'Sorry, no, y-yes...' she stammered. 'Come in.' She stepped back as he brushed past her into the hall. She closed the door and turned to face him, and it took all her self-control to say coolly, 'Though I can't imagine what you and I have to talk about, Mr Aristides.'

Why was Aristides here? Had Delia finally told her family the truth? But if so why hadn't she called and told Helen? Suddenly not having heard from Delia for so long took on a frightening aspect. She had been worried for young Nicholas, but now she was more worried for her friend.

'Nicholas.'

'You know!' Helen exclaimed and lifted shocked violet eyes to his. 'So Delia finally told you,' she prompted with a sinking heart.

She had always known that when the time came Delia would reveal to her family that Nicholas was her son and take over the full-time care of the boy, but she hadn't expected it for at least another three months. Nor had she fully expected the extent of the pain in her heart at the prospect of becoming an honoured aunt, a visitor in Nicholas's life rather than virtually his sole carer.

'No, not Delia,' he said curtly. 'A lawyer.'

'A lawyer...' Helen was hopelessly confused and the mention of the legal profession filled her with foreboding. To give herself time to gather her scattered thoughts she crossed the hall and opened the door to the large cosy sitting room. 'You will be more comfortable in here.' She indicated one of the two sofas that flanked the fireplace, where a fire burned brightly in the grate.

'Please take a seat,' she said politely, nervously clasping her hands together in front of her. 'I'll get you a coffee, you must be cold. It is a foul day.' She noted a droplet of water fall from his thick black hair to linger on the slant of his cheekbone. 'And you need a towel.' She was rambling, she knew, and quickly she turned and scurried back out of the room, her legs shaking and her mind racing. She grabbed her bag off the hall table and dived into the kitchen.

Leon Aristides noted her nervousness, in fact he had noticed every single detail from the moment she had opened the door, from the hip-hugging blue jeans to the tight blue sweater that outlined her firm breasts. Her hair was much longer now, otherwise she looked no older than the first time they had met. Then she had been lovely and ripe for the plucking and he damn near had.

He had arrived at the family's island home late in the night and early the next morning had been swimming naked in the sea. Emerging out of the water he had seen her walking towards him. Her fair curly hair had framed a face that was pale with huge eyes, a small straight nose, a full lipped mouth and had been gentle in its natural beauty. She had been wearing a long-sleeved ankle-length white dress in some fine material that should have been demure but instead with the sun behind her had been virtually transparent. Beneath the dress she had been wearing tiny white briefs.

Leon shifted uncomfortably in the seat, as he again saw in his mind's eye the high, round breasts, the tiny waist, the feminine flare of her hips and shapely legs as she had moved towards him, her gaze fixed intently upon him. He had demanded who she was and what she was doing there.

Showing no embarrassment at his nudity, she had called out that she liked the early morning before the sun got too hot. But he had got hot simply looking at her, and whipped a towel around his hips as she had continued to approach him. 'I am Helen, Delia's friend from school.' And she had held out her hand and stopped not a yard away.

The thickly lashed eyes she had lifted to his had been a smoky violet, and full of hidden promise. He had been surprised and tempted to take what she had been so blatantly offering, until it had registered with him that she could only be fifteen, the same age as his sister. He had dismissed her with a few crude mocking words, disgusted with his own reaction more than with her.

When she had answered the door earlier, and looked up at him with those huge violet eyes, he had had the same urge all over again. Remarkable, because she wasn't his usual type at all; he preferred tall, slender brunettes, an image of his current lover, Louisa, a sophisticated French lady, forming in his mind. He had not seen her for two months, which probably accounted for his unexpected sexual reaction to Helen Heywood. She was the direct opposite of Louisa, a pale-skinned ash-blonde who couldn't be much more than five feet tall. Added to which the innocent-looking Miss Heywood had to be the most devious, money-hungry woman he had ever encountered, and he had encountered quite a few.

Still he had her in his sights now and she was no match for him, he concluded arrogantly and briefly closed his eyes. *Theos,* he was tired, and for a man who lived to work that was some admission, but the last few weeks had been hell.

It had started when he had taken a phone call in his office at Aristides International Bank in Athens a month ago. His father and sister had been in an accident and he could remember the day in every minute detail.

He had paced the length of the hospital corridor outside the operating theatre, with a face like thunder. None of the hospital staff who had passed him had dared to speak, but they had all known he was Leonidas Aristides the international banker, with offices in Athens, New York, Sydney and Paris, as rich as Croesus, and about to be more so after the tragic events of the day.

He had stopped outside the double doors and wondered how long it had been. He had glanced at the functional watch on his wrist, and stifled a groan—a meagre forty minutes.

Not even an hour since they had wheeled the broken body of his sister Delia through the metal doors of the operating theatre. Only three hours since the telephone call he had taken at the bank informing him of the car crash that had killed his father instantly and badly injured his sister. Even as he had been informed Delia had been transferred by air ambulance from their island home to the best hospital in Athens.

He had trouble believing what had happened. They had all spent Christmas and New Year's Eve together on the island but he had left early the next afternoon to spend a couple of weeks in New York. He had flown into Athens early that morning assuming his father and Delia had returned to their house in the city a couple of days ago and expecting to meet his father at the bank. Only to be told his father was still at their holiday home.

How the hell had it happened? he had asked himself for the thousandth time, having already demanded the same from the hospital staff and the police right up to the minister. All he had known was Delia had been driving to the harbour with their father when apparently she had lost control of the car and ended up in a ravine. As for the top team of surgeons he had demanded and got, they had been reluctant to give an opinion on Delia's chances other than to say she was critical but they would do all they could.

He had crossed to slump down in a seat facing the theatre doors, and had laid his head back against the wall and closed his eyes in an attempt to block out the reality of the situation.

His father was dead and he had known he would mourn his passing, but his sister had been fighting for her life behind those closed doors, and he had never felt so helpless in his life.

A sense of *déjà vu* had enveloped him. A different couple, a different time, and, he had prayed, a different outcome. Four years ago in June he had sat in a private hospital very like this in New York, waiting while they operated on his wife Tina after another car crash. The passenger then had been his wife's fitness instructor who had died instantly.

A bitter, cynical smile curved his hard mouth. Later the surgeon had told him sadly his wife had died on the operating table, but they had delivered the child she was carrying, a boy. For a moment he had felt a surge of hope until the doctor, who had carefully avoided eye contact with him, had added, 'Although the child was full term he was badly injured and his chances of survival are slight.' A few hours later the child had also died.

'Mr Aristides.' Leon opened his eyes and, silently praying this accident would have a happier outcome, he rose to his feet as the surgeon approached him. 'The operation was a success and your sister is now in Intensive Care.' He heaved a mighty sigh of relief, but it was short-lived as the surgeon continued, 'But there are severe complications, she has lost a lot of blood and her kidneys are failing. Unfortunately the traces of recreational drugs in her system are not helping. But we are doing all we can. You can slip in and see her for a few moments, the nurse will show you the way.'

He was still reeling from the knowledge his sister took drugs when she died two hours later.

Opening his eyes, Leon looked around the very English-looking cosy sitting room. If he had thought the fact that his sister took drugs was the worst thing she could have done in her young life he had been proved wrong yesterday.

The intelligent, educated young lady he had imagined Delia had grown up to be had been leading a double life for years with the help of Helen Heywood. A woman he distinctly remembered his sister telling him she had virtually lost touch with when she had gone to university in London.

Even for a man as cynical as him, particularly where the supposedly fair sex was concerned, the lies and the acting ability Delia had displayed over the last few years boggled the mind. He had loved his sister though he might not have shown it as he should, and her deceit hurt. For a man who never indulged in emotion and actively disdained anyone who did, it was a galling admission and he knew exactly who to blame. His sister was gone, but Miss Heywood had a hell of a lot to answer for, and he was just the man to make sure she did.

CHAPTER TWO

HELEN STOOD IN the kitchen watching the coffee percolate, and trying to think straight. Leon Aristides was here, in her home, and he knew about Nicholas. It wasn't too bad, she told herself. So he knew Delia had an illegitimate son, and obviously he knew that Helen looked after the child. Maybe Delia had finally told her father, and maybe he had consulted a lawyer and maybe he had told Leon. But it was all very odd and there were way too many maybes!

At the very least Delia might have warned her, she thought, miffed with her friend for putting her in such a position. Snatching her bag off the kitchen table, she took out her cell phone and tried Delia's number again. It was still dead.

Five minutes later, after snagging a towel from the downstairs toilet, she walked back into the sitting room carrying the coffee tray. 'Sorry it took so long.' She placed the tray on the occasional table and held out the towel.

He took it from her hand with a brief, 'Thank you,' and, swiftly wiping his face, he began drying his thick black hair. In his dishevelled state the family resemblance to Nicholas was quite startling.

Realising she was staring, she quickly sat on the sofa opposite him. 'Black or white, Mr Aristides?' she asked coolly.

'Black, one sugar and drop the Mr Aristides. Leon will do—after all, we are old friends.'

'If you say so,' she murmured, and poured the coffee, unable to get his name past her suddenly dry mouth. As for being 'old friends,' he must be joking. Lifting her head, she handed him the cup and saucer, and flinched slightly as his fingers brushed hers. Their eyes met and for a second she saw a gleam of something sinister in the depths of his that made her stomach clench, and then it was gone and he was raising the cup to his mouth.

Oddly flustered but determined not to show it, Helen took a much-needed drink of her own coffee, and, replacing the cup on the table, she said, 'Now perhaps you can tell me why a lawyer informed you about Nicholas? Did Delia finally tell her father the truth, and perhaps he contacted a lawyer?' she queried.

He drained his cup, replaced it on the table, and raised his head, his dark eyes resting on her with cold insolence. 'By the truth, I presume you mean that my crazy sister had a child outside marriage, a son that her family knew nothing about. A son that you have taken care of from birth... Is that the truth you are talking about?' he prompted, his cold dark eyes narrowing at the look of guilt that flashed across her pale face.

'That my own sister could be so devious as to deprive her father of a grandson is beyond belief, and that you with the collusion of your grandfather apparently aided and abetted her is downright shameful, if not criminal—'

'Now wait just a minute,' Helen cut in. 'My grandfather died months before he was born.'

'My sympathy, I apologise for maligning the man. But it does not make your actions any less shameful,' he said bluntly.

'The only shameful act as far as I am concerned is your father forcing Delia into becoming engaged to a distant cousin when she returned to Greece last summer. A man of his choosing, to keep the money in the family. She is not crazy, quite the reverse. Delia always knew her father would try and marry her off eventually and prepared for it,' Helen said adamantly.

'She tried to delay it as long as possible—that was why she changed the course she was taking at university after the first year, so she could extend her studies a year. And, for the same reason, once she did graduate she decided to take a teacher's training course for another year.' Helen leapt to defend her friend. She didn't like Leon Aristides and she liked even less his derogatory comment about his own sister.

'You know more than me, it would seem,' he drawled sardonically his eyes narrowing on her small face, and Helen felt inexplicably threatened.

She hesitated and lowered her lashes to hide her too expressive eyes. It was not like her to let her tongue run away with her, and she had the disturbing conviction that she would need all the self-control she possessed around Leon Aristides.

'As to that I don't know.' She gave a slight, what she hoped was a nonchalant, shrug. 'But obviously Delia has changed her mind about Nicholas or you would not be here,' she continued. 'But I spoke to her a few weeks ago and she never said anything to me. As far as I know, she still has no intention of marrying the man and only agreed to the engagement to keep her father happy until she is twenty-five in May and comes into the inheritance her mother left her. Then she has every intention of telling the whole world she has a child when her father can no longer control her.'

'She will never have the chance.' He brushed aside her stalwart defence of his sister with a few cold words.

'My God, Delia was right about you!' she exclaimed. 'You're as—'

'Delia is dead, as is my father,' he interrupted brutally,

guessing her thoughts about him, and deflecting them in the bluntest way possible.

'They were staying on the island, and Delia was driving them to the harbour when the car slid off the road and into a ravine.' He spoke emotionlessly as if he had recited it all a hundred times before. 'Father died instantly, Delia a few hours later in hospital without ever regaining consciousness.'

Helen stared at him in stricken silence. She could not believe it, did not want to believe it.

'Dead…Delia dead,' she murmured. 'It's not possible.' She lifted wide, appalled eyes to the man opposite. 'It has to be a ghastly joke.' Not half an hour ago she had been worrying because Delia had not called; now she was expected to believe she was dead.

'The accident was on the fifteenth of January and there was a double funeral three days later.'

Suddenly, like a tidal wave crashing down on her, the full horror of his revelation swamped her mind, and she knew Aristides was telling the truth. Her heart contracted in her chest, her eyes closing momentarily as she struggled to hold back the tears. But it was a futile gesture as moisture leaked beneath her lashes. She wrapped her arms around her middle in a physical attempt to hold herself together.

Delia, beautiful, brave headstrong Delia, her friend and confidante—dead.

She remembered the first time they had met. Theirs had been an unlikely friendship, the extrovert Greek girl and the introvert English girl.

Helen at sixteen had missed a lot of schooling owing to the accident that had killed her parents. Her father had worked as an IT consultant for a Swiss bank in Geneva and they had been on a skiing weekend in the Alps, when an avalanche had buried her parents and left Helen slammed against a tree chest-deep in snow. Rescued hours later, she had fractured her pelvis, but worse had lost her sight. Whether it had been snow blindness from exposure to the brilliant sun in the hours before she had been rescued, or a psychological reaction at seeing her parents killed, it had taken her a long time to recover.

She had returned to England to live with her grandfather, and slowly recuperate. Finally she had resumed her education as a day pupil at a boarding-school in the countryside near her home. She had been put in the same class as Delia although she had been two years older than everyone else. It had been Delia who had stood up for Helen when others in the class had teased her about the ugly tinted glasses she had worn at the time. From that day forward they had become firm friends and Helen had frequently invited Delia to her home for weekends. Her grandfather had been a classics scholar who spoke fluent Greek and the school had approved the outings.

When Helen had left school early to look after her grandfather, who had been left wheelchair-bound after a stroke, Delia had continued to visit right up until she had left school herself to go to university in London. They had kept in touch by telephone and the odd e-mail, but Helen had not seen Delia for two years until she had turned up unexpectedly one weekend looking pale and sombre. Not her usual confident self at all.

'Obviously the news is a shock to you and I'm sorry to intrude on your grief.' The brisk dark voice cut into her reverie, not sounding the least apologetic. 'But I came here to see my nephew and discuss his future.'

Tight-lipped and clenching her teeth in an attempt to control her grief, Helen lifted tear-drenched eyes to Leon Aristides and shivered at the aloof glacial expression she saw on his face. If this man was mourning the loss of his father and sister it certainly did not show. He was as hard as a block of granite, and suddenly fear for Nicholas and what his future would be overrode her grief.

'Nicholas is asleep upstairs. He attends nursery school in the morning and after lunch he usually has a nap,' she said truthfully, struggling to gather her tumultuous thoughts into some kind of order. Instinctively she knew Delia would not have wanted her son brought up in the same mould as her father and brother, and she needed all her wits about her to deal with the situation. 'I don't think it is advisable to wake him up to tell him his mother is dead.' She choked over the last word.

'I wasn't suggesting any such thing.' He lifted a hand and ran it through his thick black hair, and for a moment she thought she saw a gleam of anguish in his dark eyes.

Helen began thinking maybe Leon Aristides was more upset than he appeared. Suddenly she remembered Delia mentioning that his wife and newborn child had died in an accident. This must be a double blow to him—she had lost her best friend but he had lost his father and his sister—and her soft heart squeezed with compassion.

'But he will have to be told later and in the meanwhile—' Aristides rose to his feet and stepped towards her '—I want to see some proof the boy actually exists and is here,' he declared with a sardonic lift of an ebony brow.

Helen gritted her teeth at his cynical comment and any sympathy for him disappeared. 'Of course.' She stood up and found he was much too close, and sidestepped out of his way. 'If you will follow me,' she murmured and made for the door.

The curtains were closed against the dismal dark day and a small car-shaped night light that Nicholas adored illuminated the bedroom. The bed was also a model of a car, and lying flat on his back was Nicholas wearing white underpants and a tee shirt. With his curly black hair falling forward over his brow, and his thick black lashes lying gently against his smooth cheeks, he was deeply asleep.

Helen smiled down at the infant, and very gently brushed a few stray curls from his brow. She heard a deeply indrawn breath, and glanced back at Aristides. She could sense the tension in every muscle and sinew of his big frame as he stared down at the sleeping boy, totally transfixed.

Helen didn't like the man, she found him hard and cynical. If she was honest she also found him intimidating. He was not only tall, but powerfully built with wide shoulders and a broad chest, lean hips and long legs. Yet right at this moment he looked as vulnerable as the child who held his complete attention.

Silently she moved back a few steps towards the door, to give him some privacy in which to get over the shock of seeing his nephew for the first time. He was entitled to that much, but he was not necessarily entitled to sole care of the child, she reminded herself firmly.

Her eyes misted with tears as she saw again in her mind's eye Delia's face when she had turned up out of the blue on a day in February much like this one four years ago. She had been upset, but determined, and no amount of talking had been able to get Delia to change her mind.

Delia had been pregnant and unmarried at twenty. There had been no way she was going to tell her father, and she had asked Helen to help her take care of the baby until she came into her own fortune. Then she could say to hell with her father and bring her child up as she wished.

Personally Helen had thought it was the craziest idea she had ever heard, and had told her so. She had doubted Delia could keep the pregnancy hidden, never mind keeping a child secret, and what about the father?

The father was a fellow student who had been killed in the London train crash that had been all over the papers a few weeks earlier. But Delia had had it all worked out. She would go home for Easter as usual and return to university in London afterwards. Her father had been ecstatic at the news Leon's wife was finally pregnant so he would pay Delia even less attention than usual.

Delia had been convinced she could get through the holiday without anyone realising she was pregnant. The baby was due on the first of July and it would be simple to book into a private hospital in London to have a Caesarean delivery in mid-June. Then she could leave the child with Helen and still be able to return to Greece for the summer holidays without her family being any the wiser. Helen had thought the whole idea ridiculous, but Delia had been nothing if not determined.

A wry sad smile tipped the corners of her lips. Thinking about Delia now, she realised she had been just as stubborn and autocratic in her own way as her father and brother.

Even so Helen had flatly refused her request and with the help of her grandfather had tried to persuade Delia that she must tell her family the truth. Helen had thought they had managed to convince her to do just that when she had left two days later.

A strong hand grasped her arm shocking her out of her musings.

'He is every inch an Aristides,' Leon said softly, turning towards her and blocking her view of the room. 'You and I really do need to talk.' The pressure of his fingers on her arm and the closeness of his large frame did extraordinary things to her breathing. 'Are you alone here?'

She gasped and tilted back her head to lift her gaze and met his intent black eyes. Her mouth ran dry and her pulse took off at an alarming rate. He saw her reaction and his dark gaze fell to her softly parted lips and then provocatively lower to linger on the proud thrust of her breasts against the soft wool of her sweater, before flicking back up again to her face. 'You are a very attractive woman—perhaps a live-in lover?'

'Certainly not,' she snapped, blushing to the roots of her hair.

'That makes it easier,' he murmured, and settled a long finger over her lips. 'But shh—we don't want to wake the child.'

Her lips oddly tingling from the touch of his finger, before she knew what was happening she was out of the bedroom, the door closed behind her and halfway down the stairs.

'You can let go of my arm now.' Helen finally found her voice, deeply shaken by the startling effect Leon Aristides' deliberately sensual look and touch had upon her.

He let go of her arm without a word, and walked down the stairs and into the sitting room, obviously expecting her to follow. She stopped for a moment at the foot of the stairs to gather her chaotic thoughts into some kind of order. But the resentment burning bitterly in her breast did not help. Who the hell did he think he was, treating her home as if it were his own?

Unfortunately she knew exactly who he was, she recognised with her next breath; a wealthy, powerful man who happened to be Nicholas' uncle. Much as she would like to be rid of him, she realised it wasn't in Nicholas' best interest or hers to antagonise the man, and reluctantly she finally followed him into the room.

He had flopped down on a sofa, his head thrown back and his eyes closed. He had opened his jacket and loosened his tie. The top button of his shirt was undone, revealing the strong tanned column of his throat. His long legs were splayed out in front of him, the fabric of his trousers pulled tight across his thighs and graphically outlining the bulge of his sex.

Flaked out as he was, for a moment his sheer physical impact hit her like a blow to the stomach. Leon Aristides might be one very conservative banker, but there was no mistaking he was all virile male.

Her violet eyes roamed in helpless fascination over his superb body. He was probably a magnificent lover, she thought, and a shaming tide of pink coloured her cheeks.

Helen felt like a voyeur; erotic thoughts about men had never bothered her before. What on earth was happening to her? She rubbed suddenly damp palms down her thighs, and, swallowing hard, took an involuntary step back. She raised her head to find his dark, astute eyes resting on her. Oh, my God! Did he know what she had been thinking? And quickly she broke into speech. 'Would you like another coffee or something?'

'Something…' His dark eyes swept leisurely over her in undisguised masculine appreciation. Suddenly she was horribly conscious of her old denim jeans and the well-washed sweater she was wearing. But even worse was the peculiar swelling in her breasts at his lingering appraisal. 'Yes, the something has more appeal,' he drawled huskily. 'What do you suggest?' and he smiled.

Her gaze dropped from the amusement in his dark eyes to the curl of his sensual lips, revealing gleaming white teeth, and for a second she stopped breathing, mesmerised by the unexpected brilliance of his smile.

Realising she was staring again, she hastily glanced somewhere over his shoulder and blurted out the first thing that entered her head. 'Tea or wine, if you prefer? When my grandfather was alive he kept quite a lot of red wine and I don't drink much so there are a couple of bottles around.' She was babbling again, but nothing like this had happened to her before.

Helen wasn't naive. She knew all about sexual attraction— she had dated Kenneth Markham for almost a year, until he had decided to go to Africa and help the starving, and she had never heard from him again. But this was different—instant and electric—and it shocked her witless.

'I'll go and get the wine.' She dashed back out of the room like a scalded cat.

In the safety of the kitchen she took a few deep, steadying breaths. She was still in shock at the news of Delia's death, she told herself. That had to be why her body had reacted so peculiarly to Leon Aristides. She didn't even like him, and she certainly wasn't attracted to overtly macho men. She much preferred the sensitive, caring type like Kenneth, the type one could talk to without feeling threatened in any way. It had to be the tragic news that had made her hormones go haywire. A physical anomaly brought on by the pressure of the moment. Reassured by her conclusion, she took two glasses from a cupboard, before she crossed to the wine rack and reached for a bottle of wine.

'You're tiny, allow me.' She almost jumped out of her skin as a long arm stretched over her head.

She spun around to find the damn man only inches away. 'I can do that,' she said in a voice that was not quite steady. Disturbed by the ease with which his closeness affected her all over again.

'It is done.' He shrugged his broad shoulders, holding a bottle of red. 'But you can give me the bottle opener, and something to eat would be much appreciated. I was too busy searching for this place to take time out to eat lunch.' His dark eyes flicked down at her. 'Sandwiches will do,' he ordered calmly.

The 'tiny' and his arrogant assumption she would feed him infuriated her, but she didn't argue. It was a relief to move away from him and, opening a drawer, she took out the bottle opener, and slapped it on the bench beside him before crossing to the fridge and extracting a block of cheese.

'Will cheese do?' She flicked him a glance and was further incensed to see he had moved to sit at the kitchen table, a glass of wine in his hand, the bottle of wine in front of him and another glass on the table.

'Perfectly,' he said calmly and took a sip of the wine.

Turning her attention to the task before her, Helen quickly made two sandwiches and put them on a plate, all the time tensely aware of the man behind her.

'Your grandfather had good taste in wine,' his deep voice drawled appreciatively. 'In fact, according to the report my father had on him, your grandfather was a highly intelligent, highly moral, well respected professor.'

'Report!' Helen exclaimed, turning around to stare at him in amazement, the plate of sandwiches in her hand tilting precariously.

'Here, let me take that.' He reached across and took the plate from her unresisting grasp and, placing it on the table, picked up a sandwich and began eating with obvious enjoyment.

He was doing it again, ordering her around, and for a long moment she stared at him, stunned. 'Your father actually investigated my grandfather.' Her indignant gaze fixed on his hard face.

'Yes, of course,' he stated coolly. 'Before my sister was allowed to visit your home my father had checked with the school and privately that you and your grandfather were suitable people to befriend her. Obviously over the years the circumstances had changed, but neither my father nor I for that matter had any idea. Delia was nothing if not inventive.' He took another sip of wine before continuing. 'I distinctly remember three years ago a cartoon Christmas card you sent Delia particularly amused my father. He asked after you both and suggested she invite you over for another holiday. Delia's response as I recall was that your grandfather had suffered a stroke some years before and you stayed at home to look after him. It was unfortunate, but she had not seen you since she went to university in London, and apart from the occasional Christmas and birthday card the friendship had fizzled out.'

An ebony brow arched sardonically. 'I am beginning to realise my innocent little sister was like all women—as devious as the devil and an accomplished liar,' he stated witheringly and reached for another sandwich.

Helen opened her mouth to defend her friend and closed it again. What could she say? From the moment she had taken Nicholas into her home she had silently colluded with whatever story Delia had chosen to tell her family. That Delia had lied about their friendship brought the fact home with brutal clarity. But then why was she surprised? In the first few months after Nicholas was born Helen had been hoping that Delia would see sense and tell her family about the boy, while Delia had obviously been busy covering the trail that led back to Helen.

'Sit down and have a drink. You look completely stressed out,' he observed, his cold dark eyes narrowing on the look of guilt that flashed across her pale face.

She pulled out the chair and sat down, and picked up the glass with a hand that was none too steady. She lifted the glass to her lips and took a long swallow. Helen seldom drank; alcohol went straight to her head. But Aristides was right, she was stressed to breaking-point, the enormity of the deception she had agreed to finally hitting her. Much as she had loved Delia and wanted to help, Helen knew deep down inside her reasons had not been purely altruistic.

Before the death of her parents she had been a happy, confident teenager. She had had all the hopes and dreams of a young girl. School, college, a career, then love, marriage and children. But everything had altered the day of the accident. Her near idyllic life had been shattered and, much as she'd loved her grandfather, he hadn't been able to replace what she had lost.

Delia had been the one bright spot in her life, but when she had first made her outrageous proposal Helen had refused, until the sudden death of her grandfather in late April had changed everything. Delia had turned up for his funeral still pregnant and with her own family still not aware of the fact.

To Helen, grieving and totally alone for the first time in her life, Delia's request that she take care of the baby while she continued her studies suddenly had not seemed so outrageous. If Helen had been honest it was a dream come true.

'More wine?' He interrupted her thoughts, lifting the bottle of wine from the table.

She glanced at him, violet eyes clashing with black, and she knew the dream was about to become her worst nightmare. She lowered her eyes from his too-penetrating gaze and realised she had drained her glass. She also realised she needed all her wits about her for what was to follow.

'No. No, thank you,' she said with cool politeness.

'As you wish,' he replied, and refilled his own glass and replaced the bottle on the table, casting her a mocking glance from beneath heavy-lidded eyes, and then lifted his glass to his mouth.

Unconsciously she watched his wide, mobile mouth, saw the movement in the strong line of his throat as he swallowed. Her fascinated gaze followed the movement lower to where the open collar of his shirt revealed a few black hairs on the olive toned skin of his chest. Suddenly heat flushed through her veins and curled in her belly. Oh, no, she thought, it was happening again and it terrified her.

She raised her eyes to his face and opened her mouth to say something, anything, but she couldn't breathe. She simply sat there, colour flooding into her cheeks, her lips softly parted, paralysed by the sexual awareness that tightened every nerve in her body.

He replaced his glass on the table and was studying her

flushed face. He knew what was happening to her, and why. She saw his heavy-lidded eyes darken with sensual knowledge. She saw the hint of satisfaction in the slight smile that curved his mouth, and suddenly the air between them was heavy with sexual tension.

CHAPTER THREE

IT WAS THE gleam of masculine satisfaction in Aristides' lazy smile that hauled Helen back to sanity. She stiffened and clenched her teeth in an attempt to subdue the tide of heated sensation that had invaded her body. Not something that had ever happened to her before, or ever would again if she could help it.

Taking a few deep breaths, she rationalised her extraordinary reaction to the man. So she had finally realised Leon Aristides was a sexy beast, and could turn a woman on at will. But then why was she surprised? According to Delia, in her family all the men had wives and mistresses, from her great-grandfather who had started the bank, all the way down to Leon. Given that Helen was now bound to have contact with the man over Nicholas, anything of a personal nature between them was absolutely unthinkable. Nicholas' happiness was her top priority.

'Nicholas,' she said firmly. 'You want to talk about Nicholas.'

'Yes, Nicholas,' he agreed, and leant back in his chair, a contemplative look on his dark face. 'But first we must discuss Delia. Starting at the beginning is usually the most constructive way to find a lasting solution to a problem,' he offered and, much to Helen's surprise, proceeded to do just that.

'Delia was the baby of the family. I was fifteen when she was born and for the first three years of her life she was a source of joy to me. I admit after I left home to study and later to live in New York for a number of years I did not see as much of her as I possibly should have done, but I thought we had a good relationship. I saw her at least two or three times a year, usually over the holiday periods. She went a little wild as a young teenager but that was soon sorted out. My father gave her a generous allowance, and almost anything she asked for she could have.' He shook his dark head in disbelief, for once not looking the cold, austere banker Helen knew him to be.

'She always appeared content and well adjusted, so why she thought she had to hide her child from her family I will never understand.' His dark eyes narrowed speculatively on her. 'You obviously knew a different Delia from my father and I, and I guess you were a party to all her secrets.'

She looked away from his curiously penetrating gaze, and coloured slightly. 'A few.'

'How much did she pay you to keep them?'

'She never paid me!' Helen exclaimed indignantly, her colour heightened by the gleam of contempt in his eyes. 'I loved Delia; she was my best friend.' She drew in an audible breath, and lowered her head to hide the tears that threatened as memories of her friend engulfed her. But refusing to give in to her emotions, she continued.

'From the first day I met Delia at the boarding-school your father had banished her to, I would have done anything to help her because she stood up for me. I was a day pupil, which set me apart from most of the class, added to which I was two years older than everyone else.'

Leon tensed slightly at that piece of information, his dark eyes narrowing speculatively on her downbent head. So Helen Heywood was not quite as young as he had thought...interesting. He had intended to take her to court if he had to, though the thought of the resultant publicity was anathema to him. But he had forgotten how very attractive she was and now a much better scenario occurred to him.

He recalled the strange reaction of the hotel receptionist as he had enquired about the Farrow House. The young woman had looked at him rather coyly, then said, 'Of course, you must be a very good friend of Helen Heywood and Nicholas.' After seeing the child, he could guess what the girl had been thinking.

Lost in her memories, Helen was totally oblivious to her companion's scrutiny and continued, 'With the age difference and wearing glasses, needless to say the class bullies had a field-day with me. But Delia waded into them on my behalf and won. I was never bothered again.'

She lifted her head, violet eyes blazing with conviction as they clashed with astute black. 'We were firm friends from that day onward. I would have done anything for Delia, and she would have done anything for me, I know,' she said adamantly.

'Perhaps, but you never will know now,' Leon drawled sardonically. 'But carry on—I would like to know why you agreed to go along with her hare-brained scheme.'

Helen didn't appreciate the 'hare-brained' but she could not exactly deny it. If she was honest, she was amazed the deception had lasted so long. For the first year of Nicholas' life she had encouraged Delia to reveal his existence to her family, but as time had passed Helen had not been quite so eager for the truth to be told. Guilt at her own role in prolonging the situation made her voice curt as she continued.

'When Delia came to visit me four years ago, and told me she was pregnant, she had a scheme all worked out. Easter at home in Greece would be no problem; no one would notice her. According to Delia your father was over the moon because you had just told him your wife was pregnant and the much-wanted grandchild was due in August. How could she, even if she wanted to, disgrace her family and spoil everyone's delight, with the news her own child was due a couple of months earlier?' she queried sharply, so caught up in her own emotions she never saw the flash of anger in his dark eyes.

'Anyway, she didn't want to. She didn't want her child brought up to be like her father, a chauvinistic tyrant who blamed her for the death of her mother.' Leon's head did jerk at that but he did not stop her. 'She didn't think you were much better after you agreed with him to ship her off to boarding-school because of a couple of teenage flirtations.'

His mouth twisted cynically. 'Of course, you agreed with her, and it never entered your head she might have been better served if you had gotten in touch with her family.'

'No, I didn't just agree with her,' Helen retorted hotly. 'I told her to do just that.' She paused, her anger fading at the memory of what had happened next—the death of her grandfather.

'Very laudable, I'm sure, but not very believable given the present circumstances,' Leon remarked cynically.

'You are wrong. I only agreed to help her after she returned from the Easter holiday, and came here for my grandfather's funeral. She told me that no one had even noticed she was pregnant,' Helen shot back scathingly, 'which rather proved her point.'

'Regrettable. But not worth arguing over,' he opined flatly. 'We now have a young boy's future to consider, a boy without parents.' His dark eyes narrowed intently on her pale face. 'Unless you happen to know the name of the father?'

'Delia told me he was dead,' she said, avoiding his astute gaze. She had also made Helen promise never to reveal the man's identity, and she saw no reason to break her word now.

'You are sure?'

'Absolutely,' Helen said firmly, looking straight up at Leon. Delia had shown her a newspaper cutting of the train crash that had killed the man.

'Good.' She had not given him a name, which Leon was sure she knew. Miss Heywood had very expressive eyes and she had avoided looking at him when she had answered, and for the opposite reason he believed her when she said the man was dead. 'Then there is no fear of anyone appearing out of the blue to claim the boy. That only leaves you and I.'

'Before you say anything more—' Helen rushed into speech '—you should know when Nicholas was born Delia made me his guardian, with her, until he is twenty-one. It was necessary in case of emergency and so he could be enrolled with a doctor and the like, and I have the documentation to prove it.' She felt some guilt for what she had allowed to happen, but even so she wasn't about to give Nicholas up to this granite-faced autocrat without a fight.

'I'm sure you have,' he drawled cynically. 'Before I arrived here I visited a lawyer in London, a Mr Smyth, and he is in possession of Delia's last will and testament. In it she makes you a substantial beneficiary of her estate, twenty per cent to be precise, and you and I are now joint trustees of Nicholas' money, as I am sure you know.' Helen's mouth fell open in shock. 'Don't look so surprised—after all, you are now probably the best paid nanny in the history of the world, as I am sure you also know.'

There was a sinking feeling in the pit of Helen's stomach when she heard the absolute decisiveness in his tone, and she knew he was telling the truth.

'Delia left me money.' She gazed up at him in shock and saw the contemptuous expression on his hard face. 'I didn't know, and I don't want it. I love Nicholas. I agreed to be his guardian to help Delia but not for money,' she said, horrified and furious that this man could think so badly of her. 'And I find it incredible that she made you Nicholas' guardian as well, she told me she did not want Nicholas growing up like you,' she blurted out unthinkingly.

Leon's astute gaze narrowed, his needle-sharp brain instantly recognising Helen Haywood in her upset and anger had made a simple mistake. He had said he was a trustee of the boy's estate, not a joint guardian. But he had no qualms about using her assumption to his advantage. Despite her protestations, and the care she had taken of the child, she was nothing more than a little gold-digger. 'It seems my little sister said a damn sight too much and not always the truth,' he drawled. 'But never mind, it is not important. What is important is Nicholas.'

'Do you think I don't know that?' she cried. 'I have looked after him from birth; I love him as my own. Nicholas' future happiness is all I care about.'

'Excellent.' He ignored the flare of anguish in her violet eyes. 'Then you can have no objection to Nicholas coming back to Greece with me.'

'But that's insane,' she responded emphatically. 'You can't just snatch him away from here. This is the only home he's ever known.'

'Then it is way past time he got to know his own. Nicholas is Greek, and he will quickly adapt. He will enjoy living in my home with my staff to attend to his every need. He will certainly enjoy the sunny climate rather than this constant cold grey drizzle. He is an Aristides and as such will have the best education available, and will eventually take his rightful place in Aristides International.' Leon let his hard eyes sweep over her with a calculated arrogance.

'You say you don't want the money Delia left you, yet, according to the receptionist at the hotel where I stopped to book a room for the night, you are employed as a part-time carer in the crèche for the guests' children. While a very laudable occupation, it is hardly going to make you a fortune,' he mocked. 'A fortune I already have, so what can you offer Nicholas to compare?'

Seething that the superior swine had the audacity to discuss her circumstances with a total stranger, Helen had had enough. 'Money is not everything. I love Nicholas—something you, by all accounts, know nothing about.' She did some mocking of her own.

'Ah, Delia again, I presume. You should not believe everything you hear.'

'Well, your marriage was no love match, rather it facilitated the acquisition of an American bank, according to Delia.' She lashed back, her anger overriding her common sense. 'What kind of example are you going to set for a trusting, lovable young boy like Nicholas?'

'A realistic one,' he stated rising to his feet and walking around to where she sat. 'Not the kind of independent, idealistic fairy-tale view of life you and my sister adhered to.' He captured her chin between his finger and thumb and tilted her head back so she was forced to meet the savage darkness in his eyes. 'Look where love and independence got Delia and tell me I am wrong.'

Helen was speechless for a moment, her hands curled into fists in her lap in an effort to suppress the furious urge to hit him. His sister was dead, and his sneering comment was a low blow.

'Oh! And your way was so much better—you managed to lose both your wife and your child,' she snapped. 'At least Nicholas is safe, and you are the most detestable man it has ever been my misfortune to meet. I wouldn't let you look after my pet goldfish.'

As he towered over her his fingers tightened on her chin

and she thought he was going to break her jaw during the taut silence that followed. Belatedly Helen realised she had gone way too far with her personal comment on his private life. If she wanted to keep in touch with Nicholas she had to get along with this man; how, she had no idea.

Then from just inside the kitchen door a high-pitched voice yelled, 'Let go of my Helen, you nasty man.'

A ball of fury spun across the kitchen and kicked out at Leon's shin. His hand fell from her chin and he stepped back and stared down in amazement at the child clinging to his leg.

'It's all right, Nicholas.' Helen jumped off her chair and crouched down beside the boy. 'He is not a nasty man,' she said, slipping an arm around his smooth little body and turning him towards her. 'He is Mum Delia's brother and that makes him your uncle.' Nicholas' chubby arm closed around her neck and, lifting him into her arms, she stood up. 'He is a nice man,' she said, not believing it for an instant. 'And he has come all the way from Greece to see you.'

'Just to see me,' Nicholas said, his big dark eyes, so like Delia's, lifted up to the silent man towering over them. 'You're my uncle.' Then he looked back at Helen. 'My friend Tim has an uncle who stays with him and his mum, and sleeps in her bed. Is this uncle going to stay with you and me?' Nicholas asked and cast a wary glance back up at Leon.

Helen felt the colour surge in her cheeks, and for a moment she was struck dumb. The fact that Nicholas at his tender age was aware of any adult's sleeping arrangements other than her own shocked her rigid. But Aristides had no such problem.

'Yes. I would like us to stay together,' Leon confirmed, speaking for the first time since Nicholas had entered the kitchen. 'If you will let me,' he added with a smile. 'You remind me very much of my sister Delia.'

'You know Delia?' Nicholas demanded.

'Mum Delia,' Helen prompted.

'Mum Delia,' Nicholas repeated. 'She was supposed to come and see us and didn't. But she sent me a car-shaped bed for Christmas, and lots of toys.' He wriggled free of Helen's hold to stand on chubby legs and glance shyly up at Leon. 'Would you like to see them?'

Speechless with anger, Helen simply stared as Leon knelt down and took Nicholas' hand in his. How dared he tell Nicholas he was staying with them?

'I'd be delighted, Nicholas. May I call you Nicholas?'

'Yes, come on.' Nicholas tugged on his large hand impatiently.

'Wait a minute.' Helen finally found her voice. 'For a start, Nicholas, what are you doing down here? I have told you not to come downstairs on your own.'

She felt guilty as hell. With the shocking revelations of the past hour she had forgotten he was no longer in his cot but in the new bed and could get out in a second, and she had also forgotten to fasten the child gate at the top of the stairs. 'You might have fallen.'

'I'm sure Nicholas is too big a boy to fall down the stairs,' Leon declared rising to his feet. 'Isn't that right, son?'

Since when had his nephew become his son? Helen thought furiously.

'Yes,' Nicholas responded, and by the smile on his face he didn't mind being called son at all. 'What's your name?'

'Leon Aristides.' The big man grinned down at the boy. 'You can call me Uncle or Leon, or both, take your pick.'

Two minutes later she watched man and boy walk out of the kitchen to view the new bed and a sliver of fear trickled down her spine. Her protestation that Nicholas needed a drink of juice and a biscuit, their usual ritual, was brushed aside in typical male fashion by Nicholas.

'You get it ready while I show Uncle Leon my car-bed.'

Her suggestion he needed dressing was brushed aside equally bluntly by *Uncle* Leon with, 'No problem, I can mange.'

Controlling her instinct to follow the pair, she glanced around the empty kitchen with a heart as heavy as lead as the enormity of the news hit her. Delia dead and Nicholas had yet to be told.

Oh, God! She groaned and slumped down in the chair she had recently vacated. She eyed the wine bottle and for a second was tempted to drown her sorrows, but only for a second. She had to be strong for Nicholas. She owed it to her friend to make sure the boy was happy, never mind what the indomitable Leon Aristides wanted.

Rising to her feet, she picked up the glasses and washed them in the sink. No way was she going to quietly slip to the sidelines of Nicholas' life, she silently vowed. She had dealt with enough sorrow and death in her life and she was not going to let this latest tragedy beat her.

Contrary to what Leon Aristides obviously thought with his dig about money and his patronising comment about her job at the crèche, at five feet two she was not a *tiny* ineffectual woman. The 'tiny' still rankled as she picked up the bottle from the table and put it on the back of the bench. She had a core of inner strength that had seen her through a lot of adversity that would have defeated a lesser woman.

She had nursed her grandfather for four years and continued her studies at the same time, eventually enrolling for a home-study degree. A few months after his death she had taken on the full-time care of baby Nicholas and continued her studies and last year she had obtained a degree in History of Art. Plus she was nowhere near the poor little woman Aristides thought.

Her grandfather after his first stroke at the age of sixty, had sold off the fifty acres of land that surrounded their home to an international hotel chain for development while making sure they kept the house and right of way. It was his way of ensuring there was money for his long-term care and Helen.

On inheriting her grandfather's estate after his death, and the life insurance from her parents that had been held in trust, Helen was hardly penniless.

While she was nowhere near as wealthy as Aristides, the money she had invested assured her of a reasonably comfortable living and left her free to indulge her own interests. As a freelance illustrator she had already completed the illustrations for three best selling children's books, and had a lucrative deal with the author and publisher to complete the illustrations on the full series of eight, her time spent at the crèche was a personal pleasure, but her greatest love was looking after Nicholas. Under the circumstances her life was as near perfect as she could have wished. Until today.

She opened the fridge and took out a carton of juice, then reached for Nicholas' favourite plastic mug from an overhead cupboard. She placed them both on the table with the biscuit tin, and straightened up, wondering what to do next.

Quietly she walked into the hall and stood at the foot of the stairs. She could hear the murmur of voices, and then childish laughter. She wanted to go upstairs and join them, but instead she walked the length of the hall and halfway back. She stopped at the hall table and picked up the post she had dropped earlier and looked through it. A couple of circulars and a letter. She turned it over in her hand and did not recognise the sender's address but tensed as she realised it was a solicitor's firm. She read the letter three times, and then slipped it in the table drawer.

Back in the kitchen she stared sightlessly out of the

window. The finality of the situation hit her; Aristides was telling the truth. The solicitor's letter was brief but informative, simply confirming Delia was dead and Helen was a beneficiary of her will.

Sighing, she turned. She needed something to do, something mundane so she didn't have to think of what might lie ahead. Perhaps if she began preparing supper. They always had their meal about six, then bath and bed. Scrambled egg with crispy bacon and grilled tomatoes was a favourite of Nicholas' and she was reaching for the china chicken that held the eggs when Nicholas and Leon walked back into the kitchen.

'Uncle Leon likes my bed,' Nicholas said, a broad grin on his face. 'He said he is going to get me another one just like it for when we stay at his house in Greece.' His eyes were huge with wonder. 'Isn't that great?'

With a malevolent glance at the tall dark man hovering over the boy, she bent down and picked Nicholas up. 'Yes, marvelous,' Helen got out between clenched teeth and deposited the boy on his seat at the table. 'Now drink your juice and have a biscuit, while I get supper ready.' She could do nothing about the stiffness in her tone; she was so angry it took all her self-control to speak civilly.

And it only got worse.

CHAPTER FOUR

THREE HOURS LATER Helen sat on the side of Nicholas' bed and read him *Rex Rabbit and the Good Fairy*. The first book she had illustrated. Nicholas loved the stories about Rex, a rather naughty rabbit, and the fairy that helped him out of his troubles, and the original drawing of the fairy hung proudly on his bedroom wall.

Usually this was her favourite time with Nicholas. But with Leon Aristides sitting like some huge dark spectre on the opposite side of the bed listening to every word tonight was different. She came to the end of the story and nervously glanced across at him.

His dark eyes rested on her. She watched them narrow in silent command, and she knew what he meant. She glanced quickly back at Nicholas, her nerves on a razor edge.

'Now your prayers,' she murmured, smiling softly down at him. It was their usual ritual, but tonight it held only sadness for Helen. She knew she had to tell Nicholas his mother was dead. Not least because Leon had told her so earlier in no uncertain terms when Nicholas had been otherwise occupied with his toys. If she didn't he would.

The childish voice ended with, 'God bless my Helen and God bless Delia. Amen.'

'Mum Delia,' Helen murmured automatically, and was ignored.

'Oh, and God bless Uncle Leon,' Nicholas said with a grin. Then he added, 'When is Delia coming? I haven't thanked her for my bed yet.'

No time was good for what Helen had to say, but she had no choice, and, reaching out a finger to stroke his smooth cheek, her eyes moist with tears, she told him, 'Mum Delia will not be coming back, sweetheart,' and, moving, she slipped an arm around his small shoulders.

'You know she lived a lot of the time in Greece. Well, so does Uncle Leon and that is why he is here today. He came to tell us Delia was badly hurt in an accident and she died.' Her voice broke. Saying the words out loud seemed so final.

'You mean she is never coming back?' Nicholas' bottom lip trembled, and the big dark eyes so like Delia's filled with tears. 'But why not?'

Helen tightened her arm around him and snuggled him closer. 'Remember when your hamster died and you and I had a little service and I told you he had gone to heaven where he would still be able to watch you even though you could no longer see him?'

He looked up into her face and then glanced at Leon and back to Helen. 'Has Delia gone to heaven?' he asked, big fat tears rolling down his soft cheeks.

'Yes, but she will still be watching over you.'

'But I want to see her again.' He began to sob in earnest.

'Shh, it's all right,' Helen husked.

'You won't leave me like Delia?' he gasped between his sobs, his little hands clinging to her shoulders, his body shaking.

Whether he understood the meaning of death, Helen wasn't sure, or whether he was simply picking up the enormity of the news from the tension in the two adults, she could not say. She simply held him close and stroked his dark curly hair, murmuring soothing words of love and reassurance, telling him not to worry, she would always be there for him.

Eventually the sobbing ceased and Helen laid him gently down in the bed and kissed his brow.

'Promise you won't die and leave me?' he pleaded, his eyes huge in his flushed damp face. 'Promise.'

'Don't worry, my love, I will always be here for you,' Helen said softly, brushing her lips against his brow again, and she saw exhaustion overtake him as his eyes closed and she kissed the slightly swollen lids, the smooth cheeks, and tenderly placed his car-printed duvet around his shoulders. 'I promise.' And a tear dropped from her eye to his cheek. His little nose wrinkled and he sighed and slept.

Ten minutes later at Leon's insistence Helen was seated alone in the living room while he went to make coffee. She had been too emotionally exhausted to argue and now she laid her head back against the soft cushions of the sofa and closed her eyes.

Grief and guilt washed over her in waves, and her mind spun like a windmill in a gale. What a mess, and most of it of her own making. She should never have agreed to Delia's mad idea, she should never have let her own circumstances influence her judgment, but then she would never have known the deep love she felt for Nicholas. To lose him would break her heart, yet she had always known Delia would claim him one day and somehow that had never felt so bad.

'Here, take this.' She opened her eyes to find Leon looming over her with a cup of coffee in his hand. 'I've laced it with a little cognac I found in a cupboard. You look like you need it.'

She took the mug from him and raised it to her lips and swallowed down a mouthful of the hot liquid. She grimaced as the spirit caught her throat, but the warmth seemed to spread through her veins inducing a kind of calm. Slowly she sipped the refreshing brew until she had drained the cup and put it on the coffee table in front of her.

Finally she glanced across at Leon reclining on the sofa opposite. He had finished his coffee and he was watching her from beneath heavy-lidded eyes, a brooding expression on his rugged face, and she wondered what he was thinking. A moment later she found out.

'Did you mean what you told Nicholas about never leaving him?'

'Yes, of course,' she asserted. 'I know it will be difficult, and obviously I don't expect to be physically with him all the time,' she said gathering her thoughts into some kind of order. 'I understand you will want to spend some time with him. You could take him for the holidays, as I know it is a custom in your family, plus apparently you have already told him.' She couldn't resist the dig. 'Given the circumstances it is inevitable Nicholas and I will be apart for some periods, but I will still keep in touch with him by telephone on a daily basis so he will never feel I have left him,' Helen offered and thought she was being reasonable.

'I hear what you are saying, but I don't agree. I can see Nicholas is happy with you and you don't want to part with him. But as his uncle, his only blood relative, I think we should share his upbringing. Nicholas can live with me for six months of the year and you for the other.'

'Don't be ridiculous,' Helen exclaimed, her eyes widening in astonished disbelief on his darkly attractive face. 'That would be absurd. Nicholas switching home every six months, switching schools, doctors everything—only a man could come up with such an idiotic suggestion,' she declared, for once feeling superior to the arrogant devil.

His mouth hardened. 'Exactly.'

'Then why suggest it?' she queried warily, no longer feeling superior as she realised he had set her up for something, but what?

'Don't get me wrong. I think you have done a wonderful job with Nicholas, with little help from my sister, though his knowledge of the Greek language is quite good, so she did do something right. But I have noted he calls you *my* Helen. But he rarely adds the prefix Mum to Delia's name unless you prompt him. He is upset at the news of her death, but, though it pains me to say it, nowhere near as upset as he would be if he lost you. To all intents and purposes you are his mother, and I think it would be in his best interest if he stays with you.'

'You mean you agree he can stay with me?' Helen asked, hardly daring to believe Aristides could be so reasonable.

'No, I mean the boy has had a confusing start in life with you as the only constant adult and he deserves more. He deserves two parents and a stable home and I can provide that.'

For a moment she was confused, then the full import of his words hit her and her heart sank. Obviously he had a new wife.

'So you married again; I didn't know,' she murmured. Why hadn't she thought of that? A wealthy, virile man like Leon Aristides who could take his pick of women, of course he had a wife. Suddenly the possibility of losing Nicholas completely became very real. How could she possibly deny the young boy two parents?

'No, I am not married yet.'

'You have a fiancée. You mean to marry and make a home for Nicholas?' she found the courage to ask. While her heart was breaking at the thought of losing him, her own innate honesty told her she could not deny Nicholas the chance of being part of a normal family.

Leon did not answer immediately. He placed his glass on the table between them and lounged back on the sofa, his dark eyes, piercing in their intensity, focusing on her ashen face. 'No, I do not have a fiancée. But with one condition you can marry me, and we can share Nicholas' upbringing at my home in Greece.'

Helen stared at him in stunned disbelief. 'Marry you! Are you mad?' He had to be joking. She didn't like the man. But something in the ruthless curl of his mouth, in the black unfathomable eyes that held hers, sent a prickling sensation down her spine. Her heart beat like a sledgehammer in her chest. She felt again the fear she had known as a teenager the first time they had met, and she knew he was not joking.

His mouth twisted sardonically. 'I have been accused of many things, but mad was never one of them. However, you and my sister obviously were, to have hatched such a ridiculous plot and denying a child his right to grow up in the bosom of his family. I was informed when she died that Delia had taken drugs, which might account for her perverse behaviour. So do you have the same problem? I need to know before I marry you,' he demanded arrogantly.

'I certainly do not,' she exclaimed furiously. 'And I don't believe for one minute Delia did either, she was perfectly fit and healthy the last time I saw her.'

'Then you are even more naive than you look.' His night-black eyes mocked her. 'I have the doctor's report to prove it.'

Helen was stunned into silence, her mind at first rejecting the truth, and then it slowly dawned on her she had not seen Delia since last summer. Maybe the pressures of returning to live in Greece and her engagement might have led Delia into doing something so stupid. It certainly explained her erratic behaviour over the last few months. The cancelled visits and dwindling telephone calls, suddenly it all made a horrible kind of sense. Why had she not noticed something was wrong? She had failed her friend when she had needed her. 'I never knew; I never guessed,' she murmured.

'I am inclined to believe you. Preliminary investigations seem to suggest Delia only got involved in recreational drugs last year when she returned to Athens and began to socialise in the party crowd—tragically for her.'

'Surely her fiancé could have stopped her,' Helen exclaimed.

'Her fiancé was blissfully unaware of what she got up to when he wasn't around, and when he found out after her death he was horrified. His father sent him to Japan to work and get over his loss, and I would guess by now his main feeling is that he had a lucky escape,' Leon drawled. 'Delia was more devious than any of us imagined. But as she is no longer here, you now have to pay the price for your foolishness. Unless you want to traumatise Nicholas by leaving him, you will have to marry me.'

Put like that, Helen had no defence. She had failed to recognise Delia had needed help. Helen could not, would not, compound her fault by failing Nicholas as well. But marriage to Leon Aristides...

Searching for the words, she began hesitantly. 'Surely there must be some other way that would fulfil all Nicholas' needs that does not involve marriage?' she appealed to him,

Leon Aristides saw the flicker of helplessness in her violet eyes, the slight perceptible slump of her slender shoulders, and he knew he had won. 'Nicholas has just lost his birth mother—not a very good one, I will grant you,' he said dryly. 'He sees you as his mother and he needs the reassurance of your constant presence more than ever now. You have known my nephew from birth. I have not had that privilege. I am not a brute, but there is no way I will allow you to have sole custody. Marriage between us is the only answer.' And, rising to his feet, he crossed to sit down beside her on the sofa.

'Believe me, Helen, if there was any other way I would take it.' And he reached for her hand, clasping it against his thigh. 'I have married before and I have no real desire to do so again.' He let his thumb idly caress her palm. 'But for Nicholas' sake I will.'

He felt her tremble and saw the flash in quick succession of two different emotions in her huge violet eyes. The first was fear, but the second was one a man of his experience could not fail to recognise, and he felt a surge of triumph go through him. She had tried to hide her awareness of him all afternoon, but he had seen it in her hastily lowered lashes, her pink cheeks. He could feel it in the rapidly beating pulse in her slender wrist. It would be no hardship to bed the lovely Helen and his body hardened perceptibly at the thought.

But now was not the time, besides which he still had Louisa. Nicholas was his first priority, and he must not forget Helen Heywood was as deceitful a woman as any he had ever met. As she was Nicholas' official guardian and a trustee of the boy's estate, he needed her in Greece and tied to him by the legal bond of matrimony. As her husband it would be much easier to protect the boy's interests and his own.

Ever since the death of his father he had naturally assumed complete control of the company. He had dealt swiftly and fairly with the odd objection from various distant cousins who had through inheritance retained an interest in the business. He'd had everything under complete control until the discovery of Delia's new will. Suddenly Helen Heywood's involvement posed a threat—a very slight threat, it was true. But he was a man who left nothing to chance.

Lifting her hand, he folded her slender fingers into her palm and placed it in her own lap, and sat back.

'You must see, Helen, whatever personal sacrifice you and I have to make, it is the only sensible solution,' he told her with just the right amount of wry acceptance in his tone. He let his

eyes slide over her and he gave an inward smile. She was flustered, and trying very hard not to show it. 'You told me you
have no man in your life at the moment, and I am unattached,
so no one else will be hurt, except Nicholas if we don't marry
and provide a stable home for him.'

'But we hardly know each other, never mind care,' she
argued faintly, and he saw the confusion in her eyes.

His hard mouth twisted in a sardonic smile. 'Courtesy of
Delia you seemed to think earlier you know a lot about me.'
A guilty blush stained her cheeks, which didn't surprise him
in the least, he thought with a flash of anger. She had a hell
of a lot to feel guilty about, but he let none of his anger show
as he continued, 'As for me, I know you are great with
Nicholas and that is enough for me. A convenient marriage is
not that unusual, and with the goodwill of both parties can be
quite successful. We have the added incentive of Nicholas to
ensure our marriage will be amiable.'

For the count of a few heartbeats Helen simply stared at
Leon Aristides. The genuine concern in his steady gaze was
undeniable, and not something she had thought him capable
of. Maybe he was not as hard as Delia had made out, she
didn't know any more. It didn't help that she could still feel
the warmth of his thigh against her skin, the stroke of his
thumb against her palm, and she clasped her hands together
trying to control her rapidly beating pulse.

'A marriage of convenience, you mean?' She finally
managed to speak. Of course that was all he was suggesting,
and she knew it made sense, so why did she feel oddly deflated?

'Yes,' he said with a determination that left her in no doubt.
'Obviously we will have to live in Greece as my headquar-
ters are there. But there is no reason why you should not keep
this house, and visit your friends occasionally. Business takes
me abroad quite often so it won't be a problem.'

He rose to his feet and looked down at her, a hint of cynicism in the depths of his dark eyes as they held hers. 'And there is another compelling reason why we should marry. When we spend time together with Nicholas, as is inevitable, how would it look to an outsider? Nicholas is innocent and does not understand, but the first words out of his mouth when I met him were about his friend's live-in "uncle." You and I both know what connotations people put on such a relationship and I am not having him exposed to that kind of speculation on top of the fact he is illegitimate. I know in your country a child outside of marriage is quite acceptable and fast becoming the norm. But in Greece it is still frowned upon.'

Embarrassment and, yes, guilt, she acknowledged, made her blush, and she tore her troubled eyes away from his. 'Nothing can change the circumstances of Nicholas' birth.' She made a helpless movement of her hands. 'But I hadn't thought of that,' she said shakily.

'Well, think about it now, and say you will marry me.'

'I don't think I could live with myself if I let Nicholas down.'

'Good, so that is a yes.'

He was towering over her, tall, dark and formidable. She had to tilt back her head to look at him again and reluctantly she nodded. 'I suppose so.'

'You can leave everything to me.' He reached down and wrapped his large hand around her arm and hauled her to her feet. Before she could protest his dark head swooped down and she felt the firm pressure of his mouth against her own. She caught the faint scent of his aftershave mingled with clean, slightly musky male, felt the heat of his body enfolding her and the subtle intrusion of his tongue between her softly parted lips. She swayed slightly in shock as unfamiliar electric sensations surged through her, and then abruptly he released her.

'What did you do that for?' she demanded when she could catch her breath, still reeling from the effect of his brief embrace.

'Get used to it.' And the look he levelled at her held none of the concern she had noted earlier, but a cold determination that she found oddly threatening. 'As you yourself said, Nicholas is a loving boy, and for him to feel secure with us he will expect to see some signs of affection between us.' His voice was cool and edged with mockery. 'And you could use the practice.'

She lowered her lashes over her luminous eyes. From burning with heat, Helen was burning with rage and humiliation. So in the kissing stakes Leon Aristides thought she was useless. Given his no doubt vast experience of the female sex it was hardly surprising, and why was she angry? She should be thankful. Now she knew without a doubt she need have no fear of their marriage of convenience being anything more than just that.

'I must leave now.' Leon interrupted her thoughts and she glanced back up at him. 'I am staying at the hotel for the night, and I have a few calls to make.' He spoke impatiently as though he could not get away fast enough. 'But I will be back in the morning to see Nicholas, before work commitments dictate I return to Greece, but I will keep in touch. You concentrate on getting packed up here. I will arrange the wedding ceremony for two weeks on Saturday in Athens.'

Helen gasped. 'But it is already Thursday.'

'Don't look so worried. I'll call with all the details and be back to collect you both in good time. Everything will be fine.' He turned towards the door.

A knock on the door—a coded knock: one, two, and one again—stopped Leon Aristides in his tracks. He turned and lifted an enquiring brow in her direction. 'You have a late caller, it would seem—one who sounds as though he is expected.' He saw Helen's mouth curve in a genuine smile.

'Yes, he is,' she said, walking towards him.

'Who is it?'

'It's only Mick. He works for the hotel security. I'll see you out and let him in. He always stops on his rounds for a cup of tea and to check Nicholas and I are okay,' she offered and walked past him.

Two minutes later Leon Aristides climbed into his car, a deep frown on his hard face. It was a new experience for him, being ushered out of a woman's house without a second glance while a good-looking young security guard was ushered in, and he didn't like the feeling.

Still, he thought coldly as he started the car, it was no more than he had expected. Helen Heywood was a very attractive woman in her mid-twenties; it was only natural she had a sex life. Her denial earlier of a live-in lover was disingenuous, and confirmed once again her devious nature. But what did he care? She had a shapely little figure and it would be no hardship to bed her.

He was a banker first and foremost, and he had achieved what he had set out to do. Soon he would have Nicholas in his home and Helen Heywood as his wife. The family fortune would be protected and his position as head of Aristides International Bank would be indisputable. With a bit of luck he might even be able to protect his sister's name.

He stopped the car and handed the keys to the parking attendant. A smile of ruthless satisfaction curved his hard mouth as he entered the hotel. The same girl was on reception as he asked for his key.

'Did you find Helen and Nicholas?' she asked.

The girl was friendly and obviously a gossip. Leon glanced down at her name tag and his smile morphed into one of utter charm. 'Yes, Tracy, I did, and Helen is even more beautiful than I remembered; as for Nicholas, he is a delightful boy.'

He bent his dark head slightly. 'In fact I will let you into a secret; I have asked Helen to marry me and she has agreed.'

'Oh, how romantic.'

'I think so.' Leon smiled again, ordered a meal, and left. Once in his room, he opened his laptop and began to check his messages, finding an e-mail from Louisa in Paris complaining about his long absence. Louisa was a problem he had to solve quickly, and surprisingly he realised he was rather relieved at the thought.

Helen had just seen Mick out, when the telephone rang. She listened in stunned silence as Tracy congratulated her on her forthcoming marriage. Aristides had wasted no time. She was so shocked that she agreed with everything Tracy suggested without anything really registering.

Helen went to bed with her mind in turmoil. She cried into her pillow as the full horror, the finality, of Delia's sudden death finally sank in. Then she lay red-eyed and sleepless, her mind spinning at the thought of actually marrying Leon Aristides.

She must have been mad to agree; the shocking news must have momentarily short-circuited her brain, she decided as the first rays of dawn lighted the sky. However much she wanted it to be, Nicholas was not her child, and she couldn't marry Aristides simply to keep the boy. By the time she finally fell asleep her mind was made up. She would tell Leon Aristides she had changed her mind. There had to be another way.

'Come on, Nicholas, eat your yoghurt.' He was being particularly difficult this morning. She had dressed and washed him, and settled him at the kitchen table with his breakfast, but she was still wearing a fluffy red towelling robe with eyes to match.

A pealing of the doorbell made her groan. Oh, God, what

idiot called at eight in the morning? She opened the door with Nicholas at her side to see Leon standing there, looking wide awake and vibrant in the same dark suit but with a dark grey shirt and tie that made him look even more forbidding to her tired mind.

Nicholas looked warily up at the man. 'I'm having my breakfast.'

The words were superfluous as his mouth was covered in strawberry yoghurt, and Helen, after the conventional greeting, added in an urgent aside to Leon, 'I need to speak to you.'

One look was all it took for Leon Aristides to realise Helen had changed her mind. She was hovering in the hall wearing some shapeless red robe, with her hair falling in a tangled mass around her shoulders.

'I will look after Nicholas.' He kept his tone light. 'You run along and get dressed and we will talk later.' Then, dropping a brief kiss on the top of her head, he grinned down at the boy. 'Back to the kitchen for you—I could do with something to eat.'

Fifteen minutes later, washed and dressed in jeans and a pink cashmere sweater, her hair loose, Helen entered the kitchen. But she was definitely superfluous to requirements, she realised resentfully some time later.

Leon, with a skill she would not have attributed to him, had patiently overcome Nicholas' rather sombre mood. In a stroke of brilliance he had told him amusing stories of Delia as a child, making him laugh and quietening all his fears. Within an hour Nicholas had returned to his usual sunny disposition, and was chatting happily and confidently with his new uncle, totally captivated by the man. Talk about male bonding, Helen thought, watching the pair lay out a train set on the bedroom floor. How Leon Aristides had obtained one so quickly in the rural depths of the Cotswolds, she had no idea.

By the time she finally got Leon on his own for a moment while Nicholas visited the lavatory she discovered she was too late.

'Mr Aristides,' she began, glancing down at him balanced on his haunches fixing the damn train. 'About yesterday—I've changed my mind. I don't want to relocate to Greece and I don't want to marry you. We will have to come to some other arrangement,' she finished in a rush.

Leon rested his eyes on her, his gaze running over her slim shapely body, and for a moment said nothing. He saw the determination in her expressive face and something more—the slight fear she could not hide.

'Too late,' he said softly. 'I have already told Nicholas we are all going to Greece. If you want to tell him you have changed your mind, and you don't want to go with him, fine. But if you do, you run the risk of upsetting him all over again, and maybe losing him altogether, so be warned.'

'You had no right to do that,' she gasped.

Leon rose to his feet, and grasped her arm. 'I had every right; we had an agreement,' he said coldly and saw her go pale. 'I am a man of my word. You, on the other hand, like most females, don't seem to grasp the concept. But we will marry.'

'Are you fighting?' a plaintive voice asked, and the two adults both turned to look at the small boy. Leon reacted first.

Dropping back down on his haunches, he held the boy by his shoulders. 'No, we were discussing our future together. '

Helen could do nothing but watch and agree as Leon explained Helen was going to marry him, and they were going to be his new parents and all stay together in Greece.

By the time Leon had finished Nicholas was clearly a little boy whose every dream had just come true and was suffering from a severe case of hero-worship.

Not surprisingly Helen was suffering from a severe tension

headache. The man had used emotional blackmail without a moment's hesitation to secure her co-operation and, while she bitterly resented it, she was powerless to do anything about it. When Aristides, after insisting on arranging a meeting for her with Mr Smyth for the following week, finally left around noon, claiming pressure of business, she was relieved to see the back of him.

What had she done?

CHAPTER FIVE

HELEN LOOKED AT her reflection in the mirror, and almost groaned out loud. She looked like a child in fancy dress; why on earth had she given in to Nicholas? He was a little boy— what did he know about clothes?

The answer came to her as quick as a flash. She had given into him because she loved him and always would. He was the reason she was standing on her own in a huge bedroom suite in this nineteenth century mansion, set in elegant gardens overlooking a tree-lined square in Athens, about to be married to a man she didn't love, and who certainly didn't love her.

The past couple of weeks had been chaotic. Tracy and the friends Helen had made on the hotel staff had turned up at her door at the weekend and insisted on throwing a wedding shower for her. They had pooled their resources and given her a present of some skimpy lace briefs and the most revealing negligee she had ever seen, well aware of her penchant for delicate underwear. Not that Leon was likely to see her wearing them, but just the thought made her blush. If that was not bad enough Tracy had brought a bridal magazine and declared she must choose a glamorous wedding dress. When Helen had said no, it was to be a simple civil ceremony, Tracy had declared that as she was marrying a filthy rich man the least she could do was look the part, and had left the magazine behind when she'd left in case Helen changed her mind.

Which was why she now looked so juvenile. Nicholas had seen the pictures in the magazine and decided one model was wearing the exact same dress as the fairy on his bedroom wall. He could be as stubborn as a mule and she knew where he got that from, she thought dryly. He had gone on and on about wanting to see her wearing the fairy dress, until finally she had given in. On a visit to London to keep her appointment with Mr Smyth the lawyer, she had bought the gown.

Leon had telephoned frequently and visited them again earlier in the week. With ruthless efficiency he had made a deal with the hotel management to take care of her house and arranged for the transportation of all the items Helen had decided were essential for their relocation to Greece. Then he had spent most of the afternoon with Nicholas before leaving at six for a pressing engagement in Paris.

Helen had not seen him again until late yesterday afternoon. His PA, Alex Stakis, had arrived yesterday to escort her and Nicholas to Athens in the Aristides private jet. Apparently Leon had been too busy. Well, that was fine by Helen; the less she saw of him, the better.

He had the uncanny ability to make her very aware of him and, worse, aware of herself in the most peculiar way. Her body seemed to have taken on a life of its own at odds to the dictates of her brain, and she didn't like the feeling. Last night, after charming Nicholas into agreement, he had ordered an end to her early suppers with the boy and insisted she dine with him later after Nicholas was in bed. Bitterly resenting his overbearing attitude, but powerless to argue with him in front of Nicholas, she had reluctantly agreed.

Dining alone with him had been an ordeal. Leon had been perfectly polite, the conversation mostly confined to the wedding arrangements for the following day with a few social niceties thrown in. But somehow every time his dark eyes rested on her she had to battle down the embarrassing heat that threatened to colour every inch of her pale skin.

It was galling to have to admit that Leon could make her feel physically conscious of him without any effort on his part. Her only comfort was the knowledge that he wasn't in the least attracted to her. He had as good as told her so the one time he had kissed her. All she had to do was control the odd feeling of panic that he aroused in her and concentrate on Nicholas, and everything would be fine.

She glanced at her reflection again, a wry smile curving her lips. She certainly had no fear of inciting the interest of any male over the age of seven in this gown. Fashioned in silk, the sleeves were long and wide at her wrists. The bodice embroidered with silver thread skimmed her breasts and narrow waist ending in a point over her flat stomach. The skirt of the gown fell in fine panels of cobweb silk of varying pointed lengths around her ankles. Not something Helen would ever have chosen. Plus the jewel encrusted satin slippers with upturned pointed toes she wore on her feet instead of the high heels she usually favoured did nothing for her lack of height, but at least Nicholas would be happy. She was totally unaware of how the gossamer fine fabric sensuously caressed her slender body with every move she made.

The door opened and the housekeeper, Anna, a tall, grey-haired woman of about sixty, walked in, closely followed by Nicholas.

'Oh, Helen, you look beautiful.' He gazed up at her, his dark eyes shining like jewels. 'Exactly like my fairy picture.'

'Thank you, darling.' She bent down to give him a hug.

'Uncle Leon sent me to get you 'cause it is after two,' he said, puffed up with importance. 'Everyone is waiting.'

Anna looked at her. 'He is right, madam, and there has been a slight change of plan. The ceremony is to take place inside instead of in the garden,' she said with a telling glance at the rain lashing the window.

Helen smiled. So much for Leon's assertion that the sun always shone in Greece. 'That's fine,' she reassured Anna, glad that at least she spoke excellent English. The other members of staff she had met last night did not.

'Lead on, Nicholas.' She grinned down at him and taking his hand in hers, she headed for the door.

Standing in the hall, Leon greeted the last guests, and glanced around the group of about thirty people. He had invited only those friends and business colleagues that he deemed absolutely necessary. To the distant relatives and acquaintances he had excluded, he had used the valid excuse of the recent deaths in the family as the reason for keeping the ceremony small and low key. At some later date he knew he would have to host a party to introduce Helen and Nicholas, but right now business came first. His priority was to make sure his marriage to Helen Heywood was completed without a hitch and she was legally tied to him as his wife. For that he did not need a great show. He had already had the huge society wedding with Tina; he didn't need another one.

He moved to speak to his PA, Alex Stakis, who was also acting as his witness, and was suddenly aware of the strange silence that had fallen over the assembled guests. His PA was staring straight past him, an expression of avid male appreciation lighting his face. Leon turned and followed the line of Alex's gaze and stiffened.

Descending the marble staircase was a vision of loveliness, a girl that looked as if she had just stepped out of any red-blooded man's dream. Helen Heywood, his soon-to-be wife, and the knowledge sent a surge of pleasure through his powerful frame that had nothing to do with business and everything to do with the tightening in his groin in anticipation of the night ahead.

Her ash-blonde hair was loose and fell in ringlets around her slender shoulders. Her gown was a fantasy in white and silver, long-sleeved with a deep vee neckline that revealed the creamy curves of her breasts, and faithfully followed every exquisite line of her body. The skirt skimmed her hips and floated in a stream of flimsy panels around her legs and thighs revealing tantalising glimpses of pale flesh as she descended the marble staircase. Her small feet were encased in harem styled slippers and to top it all off on her head was a silver garland of tiny rosebuds. She was laughing down at the little boy holding her hand and he was grinning back.

For a long moment Leon simply stared, and he had a fleeting sense he had seen Helen like this before. But he couldn't have, she looked ravishing, and he certainly had not seen her wearing make-up; even though she wasn't wearing much, the effect was stunning.

Her sparkling violet eyes were accentuated by a misty shadow and a touch of mascara exaggerated her incredibly long lashes. Her full lips were coated in a deep rose gloss and her pearly white skin was tinted by the faintest of natural blushes. She looked bewitching, the perfect bride. Innocent, and yet sensual, and the way the flimsy material clung to her petite body was as sexy as hell.

But she also looked as out of place in the small, sophisticated civil ceremony he had arranged as snow in summer, he realised grimly and frowned.

He had told her it was to be a simple ceremony, and it had never occurred to him she would dress as a bride. But this was her wedding, the only one she was ever going to have if he had his way, and he always did.

Inexplicably Leon felt guilty. His mouth tightened as he walked forward, his eyes focused on her lovely face. 'Helen you look beautiful,' he stated, and bared his teeth in a smile.

'Thank you.' She glanced at him and didn't bother to return the smile. Instead she immediately gave her attention to the little boy holding her hand. 'Nicholas chose my dress, didn't you, darling?'

A wry smile quirked his mouth. If that was true the boy had a heck of a precocious view of the female form for one so young. Then abruptly he stiffened as he saw more of her breasts than was safe in his semi-aroused state. And the luminous look of unconditional love in her eyes as she bent towards the boy as he cheerfully agreed didn't help his condition.

No woman, not even his own mother, had ever looked at him like that. Not that he would want them to, he thought cynically. He had all he wanted, or he would have tonight, he amended, and reached for her hand, enfolding it firmly in his own. 'The celebrant is waiting.'

Helen listened to the bearded little man reel off the service in Greek with a little English thrown in for her benefit and responded appropriately, not looking at Leon unless she had to. When he had taken her hand at the foot of the stairs she had felt a sudden quickening in her pulse and almost panicked. But one glance at his set face, his broad shoulders and solid, muscled body immaculately clad in a sombre dark suit had been enough to calm her nerves.

Leon Aristides looked about as happy as the condemned man heading for the electric chair, his attempt at a smile a mockery. However, this was a marriage of convenience, they had both agreed, so she had nothing to worry about.

Finally when the gold band was firmly on her finger, and

surprisingly a gold band on Leon's as well she heaved an inward sigh of relief. Then the little man instructed Leon to kiss his bride.

Leon took her chin in his hand and tilted her face up to his. Their eyes met and for an instant she saw a flare in the ebony depths of his that made the hairs on the nape of her neck stand on end. It took all her self-control not to flinch when his dark head lowered and he brushed her lips briefly with his own.

'Now that wasn't as bad as you expected,' he said softly, his eyes gleaming with sardonic amusement as he curved an arm around her waist and turned her to face the guests, well aware of her initial reluctance.

And it wasn't so bad, Helen conceded a few hours later. She had managed to control her urge to flinch every time Leon looped an arm around her waist, reminding herself it was nec- essary for Nicholas' sake. If she had to grit her teeth occa- sionally to subdue the little nervous tremors that afflicted her when he laid his hand on hers at the table or touched her cheek in an apparently affectionate gesture for the benefit of the guests, nobody seemed to notice. And after a long, leisurely meal and two glasses of champagne Helen was convinced she was over the worst and her self-confidence was restored.

Alex Stakis had made a speech, and Leon had said a few words, and then the party had moved from the dining room into a huge drawing room and become more informal.

She had met Leon's friend and lawyer, Chris Stefano, and his wife Mary who was English and also a lawyer before her marriage. Helen liked her and quickly discovered Mary was the proud mother of an eight-year-old boy, Mark, and twins, a boy and a girl who were the same age as Nicholas, and, as they were all bilingual, the children quickly made friends.

Alone for a moment, Helen allowed herself a sigh of relief. Thankfully Leon had finally left her side and was deep in discussion with Chris Stefano and another man. She glanced around the room. Sophisticated, elegant people stood around in groups chatting and drinking. Not really her scene at all, and thanks to Nicholas she was hopelessly overdressed.

'You look a little lost.' Mary Stefano approached her. 'Don't worry, you will get used to it,' she said with a glance across to the group of men. 'I have been married to Chris for nine years and in all that time I have never been to a party, wedding or baptism where the men haven't ended up discussing business, especially Leon and Chris.' She grinned.

'I can see that.' Helen smiled back.

'Well, look on the bright side—at least you will have Leon to yourself on the honeymoon.'

'We're not having a honeymoon,' Helen declared quickly, the very thought made her inwardly shudder. 'Leon is far too busy, and I have to take care of Nicholas.'

'Not much of a wedding night with your son around to wake you at the crack of dawn.'

'Oh, Nicholas is not my son,' Helen declared swiftly. 'He is Delia's child, but I have always helped to look after him while she studied.' A sad smile curved her lips. 'Now with Delia gone—'

'Delia's, you say?' Mary cut in and gave her an odd look. 'I see, well, I'd better go and find my brood. It is almost seven, time we left.'

Puzzled by Mary's comment, Helen paused for a moment. Surely Leon must have told his friends Nicholas was Delia's child. She was about to follow Mary and ask her, but before she could move the celebrant appeared at her side and began a long conversation in a mixture of English and Greek. Good manners dictated she stay and listen. Her own command of Greek was slight, only what she had picked up from her grandfather and Delia when she had been teaching Nicholas.

He, on the other hand, being so young, had grasped the language remarkably well, and Helen had no doubt after a few weeks living in Greece he would be speaking it like a native.

Finally the celebrant left to refill his glass and Helen turned towards the door, intending to look for Nicholas.

'Helen.' A long arm snaked around her waist. 'Going somewhere?'

She stiffened automatically and tilted back her head to glance up into the hard face of Leon. 'I'm going to find Nicholas, it is past time he was in bed.'

'There is no need. Mary and Chris are taking him to stay at their house for the night.'

'Whatever for?' And not giving him time to respond, she said swiftly, 'Nicholas has never been away from me for a whole night before.' She felt his hand tighten on her waist and saw the mockery in his dark eyes and suddenly the old tension Helen felt around him returned.

'Then it is about time he was. I know you love him, but you are in danger of smothering him,' he told her bluntly. She opened her mouth to object but he cut in dryly, 'Before you say anything else, Mary offered to take him after *you* told her we had no honeymoon planned. Nicholas is delighted at the idea, and here they come.'

Helen walked into her bedroom and closed the door behind her. It was over. She pressed a light switch and the room was dimly illuminated by a couple of bedside lamps. For the first time in over three and half years there was no Nicholas to check on, and the knowledge was saddening. From being virtually the centre of his universe she had to accept he was growing up; his life, his horizons, were expanding, which was as it should be.

Leon had been right about Nicholas; with a kiss and a hug

for Helen, he had left happily with Mary and her family. It had taken another few hours and another buffet-style meal before the final guest had departed, and she had been left alone with Leon. She had refused his offer of a nightcap pleading exhaustion, which wasn't far from the truth.

Sighing, she pulled the garland from her head, a brief smile curving her lips. Well, at least Nicholas had got his wish. She walked into the huge *en suite* bathroom that was bigger than her bedroom at home. Along with the usual luxurious fixtures there was a huge circular spa bath almost big enough for her to swim in.

Helen slipped out of the dress and her briefs, dropping them on the floor. She piled her hair into a shower cap, and took a quick shower, before wrapping a huge bath sheet sarong-style around her naked body. She crossed to the double vanity basin where she had left her toiletries and picking up a brush, swiftly brushed the carefully contrived ringlets out of her hair until it fell in its usual soft waves around her shoulders. No sign of a bride remained, she thought, tucking her hair behind her ears, and picking up her discarded briefs, she dropped them in the laundry bin before gathering up her dress and entering the adjoining dressing room.

They were the only rooms, plus the nursery suite across the hall that was Nicholas' that she could safely say she knew how to find. Tomorrow morning she really must get Anna to give her a guided tour of the house. There had not been time yesterday and today she had merely gone where she was told.

Helen opened the closet where her clothes had been stowed with Anna's help the night before and hung the dress up. Opening a drawer, she ignored the flimsy negligee and withdrew a knee-length cotton nightshirt she usually wore around Nicholas. A tender smile curved her lips as she glanced at the print of the two teddy bears on the front. Nicholas had

told her the first time he had seen her wearing it that the shirt
made her look doubly cuddly.

She was smiling as she wandered back into the bedroom,
and tripped over the bottom of the bath sheet.

'Careful.' Two strong hands grasped her shoulders and
steadied her. 'There is no need to kneel at my feet just yet,' a
deep voice drawled mockingly.

'You!' she exclaimed, looking up into the amused dark eyes
of Leon. 'And I wasn't,' she snapped, shrugging his hands off
her shoulders and stepping back. 'This sheet is too big.' And
so was he.

Helen's heart skipped a beat as her startled gaze swept over
him. His tall, lithe body was clad in only a black towelling
robe that exposed a large area of hair darkened chest and
ended mid-thigh, revealing his long legs. For a banker, a man
who did no physical work, he had a magnificent physique, the
thought came unbidden to her mind.

Then suddenly she realised the only thing protecting her own
naked body was a towel—a towel that, following her tripping
over it, had slid perilously south. She dropped her nightshirt and
hastily hauled the bath sheet as far up as it would go.

'This is my room and I would like you to leave,' she
declared a little shakily.

'It is also mine, the master suite,' Leon said with a soft,
husky laugh and she was struck dumb by his outrageous dec-
laration. Before she could even get her head around the fact,
never mind object, his strong hands spanned her waist and he
swung her off the floor.

With her feet dangling in the air, she instinctively reached
out and grasped his broad shoulder to steady herself. With her
free hand she hung onto the knot in the towel as if her life
depended on it. She had never been on eye level with him
before, his face suddenly only inches from her own. Her

shocked gaze met the glittering intensity of his night-black eyes and her heart lurched in panic. Her position had just become a heck of a lot more perilous, she realized, swallowing hard. His hands were burning into her waist, and her breathing was suddenly erratic.

'What on earth do you think you are doing?' Red-faced with embarrassment and something more she refused to recognize, Helen tried to wriggle free. 'Put me down.'

'Certainly.' He moved and somehow instead of his hands on her waist one long arm held her clasped firmly against his big body. His other hand twisted in the waving mass of her hair, tipping her head back.

She stared at him like a mesmerised mouse. She saw his dark head lower. He wouldn't...he couldn't be going to kiss her...

'But first...' Even as her own lips trembled in expectation of his kiss his firm lips brushed the tender skin of her throat.

The warm moist flick of his tongue seared her skin, sending a starburst of tiny tremors racing along every nerve in her body. His sensuous mouth closed over the suddenly racing pulse in her neck and paused to suck lightly before trailing a string of kisses up her throat in a slow, seductive path to her lips.

'No.' Helen choked and tried to resist but a strange warmth began to unfurl in the centre of her being, her body betraying her as a rising tide of totally new emotions flowed through her.

'No,' she murmured again, but it was more of a moan, her lips helplessly parting beneath the heady pressure of his mouth to accept the subtle penetration of his tongue. His hand tightened on her nape and he kissed her with a slow, seductive passion that stoked the unfamiliar warmth into a flame that seemed to melt her bones. She had never known a kiss could be so exquisite she thought dreamily, never known anything so pleasurable existed.

She sighed when he broke the kiss, and groaned as he bit

the soft lobe of her ear, his warm breath curling around the inner whorls.

'Do you still want me to put you down?' His deep, husky voice resonated through every cell in her body.

Helen stared dazedly into the smouldering blackness of his deep set eyes, and the temptation of total capitulation to the unknown pleasure he was offering urged her to say no. His hand at her nape stroked down to splay over her bare shoulder blades holding her close to the muscular wall of his chest, her breasts inexplicably tightening at the contact. His mouth covered hers again and he was kissing her as she had never been kissed before, deeply, erotically. She shuddered and clung to him, the flames of desire burning ever higher, and when he finally lifted his head she was helpless against the storm of heated sensations roaring like wildfire through her.

He lifted his head and drawled thickly, 'Well, Helen, must I put you down?'

The 'no' of surrender hovered on the tip of her tongue. His hand slipped down and drew her into the hard heat of his lower body. Crushed against him, she felt the rigid length of his masculine arousal against her churning stomach, and in a moment of clarity she realised what she was inviting.

'Yes. You—you...' She panicked, and, lost for adequate words, she shoved her hands against his chest and began to struggle like a deranged idiot. 'You animal.'

Something deadly flickered in the depths of his eyes, then it was successfully masked. 'All right, I heard you,' he drawled mockingly and lowered her to the floor.

CHAPTER SIX

HOT AND FLUSTERED, Helen staggered back a few steps and frantically tried to assimilate what Leon had just said and done and why. He had told her she was hopeless at kissing, she wanted to yell at him, her body strumming with the opposing emotions of fury and a frustration she had never experienced before.

He had said their marriage was one of convenience…but whose? She asked the question she should have asked herself the minute he'd suggested marriage. Certainly not hers. She had left her home and come to live in a foreign country to accommodate him and his lifestyle, and if he thought for one second she was going to accommodate him in bed as well he was in for a rude awakening.

She grasped the bath sheet tightly around her. 'What do you think you are playing at?' Her eyes blazed a brilliant violet up to his. 'Ours is a marriage of convenience and don't you forget it.'

'A convenient marriage, yes, but also a legal marriage, and as such you must know it is usual to consummate the union.' His dark cynical gaze held hers and she stared back in appalled amazement. 'If anyone is playing around here it is you.'

'Me?' she screeched. She could not believe the turn of events. 'Are you out of your mind?'

He shook his dark head dismissively. 'Oh, come on, Helen,' he drawled as he lessened the space between them. 'Who do you think you are kidding? I am no fool. Your earthy little moans, the soft flush of arousal colouring your skin are a complete give-away,' he declared throatily, and reached out to brush a strand of hair over her shoulder, not the least fazed by her angry outburst. 'You want this just as much as me. In some cases I believe a bit of game-playing can spice up a jaded sex life, but in our case it is not necessary, I can assure you.'

Helen stilled, her eyes widening in confusion on his ruggedly attractive face. She could not believe what she was hearing. His strong hands curved over her shoulders and he stared down at her, his firm lips curling in a knowing, sensual smile, all confident, virile male.

'I will make it great for you, believe me.'

It was his colossal conceit that finally got through to her and from being confused she was instantaneously contemptuous. 'No, you arrogant jerk.' She hissed like a spitting cat and shoved him hard in the chest, catching him unawares and ducking free from his hands.

His face darkened, all traces of humour vanishing from his granite-like features. 'It is a bit late for outraged virtue,' he drawled derisively, his dark eyes narrowing on her flushed furious face. 'You can't pretend you are an innocent, Helen. You are an adult woman, with a woman's needs. True, Nicholas might have curtailed your love life a little, but I saw the very convenient arrangement you had with Mick the security guard. And as for the outfit you wore today, it simply screamed sex. So no more games.'

He thought Mick was her sexual partner, and her fairy styled dress was sexy. She almost laughed out loud. The man must live on another planet. She shook her head in amazement at his misconceptions. 'I am not—' was as far as she got.

'Oh, yes, you are.' He looped an arm around her waist and deftly swept the towel from her body.

For the first time in her adult life she was totally naked in front of a man, and the shock held her rigid. Protectively she closed her eyes against the flush of embarrassment colouring her skin and instinctively she leant away from him. But that was a mistake.

'Exquisite. Helen of Troy could not have been more beautiful.' She heard his deep-throated murmur and her eyes slowly opened.

'All my fantasies in one perfect little package,' he husked, his incredibly dark eyes lifting briefly to hers and she was paralysed by the intensity of his gaze as he subjected her to a slow, raking appraisal.

For what seemed an age he just looked at her. Then his hand lifted and the pad of one finger traced the upper curves of her breasts and the valley between with a tactile sensuality that stopped her heart. She drew in a much-needed ragged breath. How could such a slight touch be so seductive? she wondered desperately. But in a second her desperation turned into helpless capitulation as he urged her closer. Her body leapt in response at the brush of his naked thighs against her own, her legs suddenly losing the power or will to support her as she swayed against him.

Her breasts felt oddly swollen, and a heady sensation seemed to thicken and slow the blood flowing through her veins. His long fingers splayed to cage the fullness of one breast in the palm of his hand and slowly, very slowly, trailed to the burgeoning rosy tip to nip ever so gently.

He murmured something in Greek but she barely heard as he delivered the same erotic delights to her other breast. A stomach curling thread of exquisite sensation pulled from her breasts to the juncture of her thighs and obliterated any lin-

gering will to resist from her mind. She moaned low in her
throat as a sensory pleasure she had never felt in her life
before totally beguiled her.

His mouth replaced his fingers, and from new sensations
of wondrous pleasure she was transported into the realms of
aching need as she felt the flick of his tongue on her breast,
his lips curling over the rigid peaks to suckle and savour each
in turn. She gave an audible gasp, her back arching involun-
tarily as he gathered her closer still, trailing a line of fire from
her breasts to her lush mouth.

'Ah, Helen, you are beautiful and responsive, everything
a man could want,' he whispered softly against her lips, taking
possession of her mouth with a deep kiss, his tongue probing
with a skilful eroticism that was nothing less than a deliberate seduction of all her senses.

She closed her eyes, her hands of their own volition
stroking over his broad shoulders and wrapping around his
neck in complete surrender to the magic of his mouth. As if
it was a signal he had been waiting for he scooped her up in
his arms and carried her to the bed.

Her lashes lifted, her huge violet eyes met the smouldering intent in his, and for a brief confusing moment she
wondered what was happening to her. He laid her on the bed,
and shrugged off his robe, and her wonder changed to awe.

His body loomed over her, outlined in the glow of the
bedside light. Naked, he was magnificent. Tall and golden, his
broad chest shadowed with black body hair that arrowed down
the centre of the hard muscles of his abdomen to widen and
frame the proud strength of his fully aroused sex. Helen gazed
almost with fear but mostly in helpless fascination, and when
she lifted her eyes to his face she saw the slow, sensual burn
in his smile as he lay down at her side.

'You look as though you have never seen a naked man

before, and yet we both know you have.' He chuckled and leaning over her he caught her hands in one of his and placed them above her head. 'But it is still a hell of a turn-on,' he husked, his dark gaze roaming leisurely over her naked body, his free hand stroking down over her shoulder to cup her breast.

She didn't know what he was talking about and suddenly fear overtook her fascination. 'You mustn't,' she breathed, like someone waking from a dream. 'You can't,' she cried, but her cry turned to whimpering moan as he lowered his head and sucked a taut nipple into the heat of his mouth again, while his long fingers toyed with the other.

He lifted his dark head. 'I can and I must. I promised you it would be great, *ma petite.*' He squeezed her breast and rolled the rigid tip between finger and thumb, tugging ever so slightly until a helpless groan escaped her.

'And for that I must take you slowly.' His dark head bent and his skilful mouth tormented and teased one breast and then the other before returning once more to take her mouth in a kiss that was a deliberate sensual onslaught designed to drive her mindless with pleasure, while his hands continued to caress her aching breasts.

'You like me playing with your breasts,' he taunted softly, raising his head, his dark eyes skimming down her writhing body. 'I wonder how much more your perfect little body enjoys.' His fingers traced the fine scar low on her belly. 'Appendix?' he prompted.

Helen tensed; should she tell him? But even as she pondered her answer his dark eyes lifted to hers.

'Ah, Helen.' The hand holding her wrists stroked down her arm and a thousand little nerves quivered at his touch. 'No need to be embarrassed; so much perfection needs an endearing blemish.' And he flicked her lips with his tongue, a glimmer of humour in his teasing caress.

Then with slow deliberation he kissed and licked his way down her throat, his strong hands forming and caressing her hot little body with a teasing tactile skill that made her burn. He nudged apart her legs and settled between her thighs, his dark head trailing lower to taste her aching breasts yet again, and down over her navel until his lips traced the slim white scar. The slightly rough scrape of his jaw against her soft skin was electrifying and she gasped and writhed beneath him, hungry for more.

Deep in her mind the thought of resistance flickered and died as she felt the heat of his mouth glide lower, his fingers touch the curls at the apex of her thighs. Her pelvis arched instinctively and she was lost, lost to everything except the incredible urge to lose herself in the drugging excitement, the hunger consuming her.

But Leon refused to be hurried. His hand traced her inner thigh and down her trembling legs, but avoided the one place where she ached for him.

Helen's hands were now free to lash out at him, but she no longer had any desire to, utterly captive to the wildly exciting pleasure he aroused in her. She reached for his broad shoulders, her fingers delighting in the sleek, smooth feel of his skin. And when he lifted his head to take her mouth again she welcomed his kiss, her tongue twining with his in a greedy, untutored passion.

The clear male scent of him filled her nostrils. The expert touch of his mouth and hands, and the breathtaking eroticism with which he continued to explore her body, incited a fevered response in her she could never have imagined herself capable of. Hesitantly she drew her fingers down the indentation of his spine to his firm buttocks, then up over his belly to his chest. Her fingers curled in his body hair, audaciously scraping the pebble-like male nipples. She heard him groan and bit lightly where her fingers had been, felt his great body jerk, and, fascinated by the discovery she could affect him, she greedily raked her hands and nails over the hard sleek muscle and sinew of his magnificent body.

For Helen place, time and reality ceased to exist. She was totally consumed by the man and the torturous pleasure he aroused in her to the exclusion of all else. She moaned when his long fingers finally parted the velvet lips of her sex and found her hot, wet and wanting. The subtle mastery of his fingers stroking and exploring the moist centre of her femininity made her groan out loud as she experienced for the first time in her life the incredible tightening sensation, the intense build up of physical pleasure that the most intimate touch of a man could arouse.

'You want me?' Leon demanded, teasing her swelling bud with his fingertip. He needed to hear her say the word although he knew the answer with every tremor, every moan that escaped her lush mouth as he skilfully deepened the rhythmic pressure until she writhed beneath him like a wild thing.

With a shaking hand he donned protection. He was rock-hard with the need to be inside her, and he stroked her again and saw her violet eyes purple with desire. She was amazing, her perfect little body a firehouse of passion, and he didn't think he could hold out a second longer. 'Say the word, Helen.'

'Yes, yes,' she moaned.

Only then did he lift her and in one fluid movement thrust into her. She was small and tight and as he surged inside her he felt the unexpected resistance and heard her cry of pain. With every muscle and sinew in his body straining with a super human effort of control, Leon managed to still inside her. He covered her mouth with his, absorbing her cry, kissing her long and deep.

Helen went from frenzied to frozen in a second. Her body

arched in an instinctive attempt to throw him off, and she tried to bite his tongue, her only thought to escape.

'Stop it, Helen, don't fight me,' Leon husked against her lips. 'Trust me.' His hands flexed and gentled on her hips, and he withdrew ever so slightly and advanced again a little more.

Incredibly Helen had still been a virgin. His wife a virgin and, along with an overwhelming need to possess her completely, he was aware of a shockingly basic feeling of primitive male posession. She was his and only his. Using all his considerable experience, he stroked and caressed her. His tongue searched the moist interior of her mouth with a sensuality that reflected what he ached to do with her body. Knowing he had to give her time to accept him.

'No, don't,' she moaned.

'Shh, Helen,' he husked softly against her mouth, his hand stroking up her trembling body to cup one lush breast. 'I promise seconds from now you will be begging me to continue.' He ran the tip of his tongue slowly around the outline of her mouth before seeking again the hot sweet passion within, while his agile fingers teased the tip of her breast.

A moment later Helen realised Leon was right. Miraculously the pain subsided and a quiver of renewed pleasure lanced through her as he continued to kiss and caress her. With a subtle thrust of his hips he moved in her, slowly stretching and accustoming her to his thick fullness, arousing her with ever-lengthening strokes.

Helen was quickly oblivious to everything except the strength, the power of him filling her, driving her inexorably once more to that torturous brink of ecstasy she could only imagine. She clung to him as though he were her world. Then with one deep, powerful thrust he sent her over the edge, her body convulsing around him in a tidal wave of earth-shattering mindless delight. She cried out his name, her legs locking fiercely around his waist, never wanting to let him go, never wanting the cataclysmic feeling to stop. She felt him tauten and heard his answering cry as his great body shuddered violently with the powerful force of his own orgasm.

His weight pinned her to the bed, but it was a weight Helen relished as the tempestuous waves of their loving gradually subsided, bringing her quivering body down to a state of languorous fulfilment.

She gazed up at her lover—her husband—utterly awestruck. Nothing she had experienced, or imagined, in her life had come close to the intense, raw emotion he had aroused, the overwhelming power of his possession.

'Leon, I never knew, never imagined,' she murmured, 'making love could be so intense, so mind-blowing—pure magic.' She smiled a slow soft curl of her lips and reached out a finger to trace the outline of his mouth.

'Leon,' she husked softly. 'Leon.' From never calling him by name if she could help it, now she wanted to shout it from the rooftops.

His name on her lips was a sensual invitation but, mindful of her recently lost innocence, one Leon knew he should not accept. But amazingly his body was telling him otherwise, and abruptly he rolled off her.

'Helen,' he responded with humorous indulgence, and, leaning up on one elbow, he surveyed his beautiful wife's slender body, her tousled mass of silken hair, and soft, swollen-mouthed, blissful smile.

God! She was good—better than good, amazing. How he could have thought she was not his type was unfathomable to him now. She was everything a woman should be and the urge to kiss her lush lips and start all over again was incredibly instant.

Accustomed to sophisticated women who knew the score and to whom having sex was not much more than a pleasurable workout, he found it a novel experience to see genuine wonder in her huge violet eyes, and Leon almost succumbed. In all his thirty-nine years he had never known a woman like her, an innocent and a sensualist rolled into one. Then cynically he reminded himself she might be innocent in the sexual stakes, but in every other way she was as cunning as the rest of her sex.

Still, it was a terrific ego trip to know he was her first, and with that in mind his conscience told him he needed to give her time to recover, though his body was telling him otherwise. His dark eyes narrowed speculatively on her lovely face. She was made for sex, as of today she was his, and there would be plenty of other times.

With that happy thought uppermost in his mind he told her, 'You are now my wife.' A smile of sheer masculine satisfaction glinted in his dark eyes. 'You are also full of surprises. Who would have imagined a sexy little lady like you, still a virgin?' He shook his head in amused amazement, and slid off the bed to stand looking down at her. 'I'm flattered you enjoyed your first taste of sex, Helen, and I must confess I am delighted to discover you have a remarkable natural aptitude for the act.' And, turning, he headed for the bathroom before he lost control and succumbed to the temptation she offered and joined her in bed again.

He disposed of the condom and washed his hands. Another bonus with Helen, he thought complacently, after years of protection, he need never use another condom as he introduced her to every aspect of sex. His big body tightened at the prospect. He glanced into the mirror above the basin and rubbed his hand against his cheek, her skin was as soft as silk, and he could do with another shave. A wry grin twisted his mobile mouth. Not tonight, though—a rough chin might help him control his basic urges in consideration of his very new wife. He had a lifetime to enjoy the pleasures of the flesh with Helen, and surprisingly the idea of being tied to one woman for years did not faze him at all.

Helen's dreamy gaze followed his retreating form as he headed for the bathroom, all long, lithe, muscular male. Her eyes widened in disbelief as the scratches on his back and tight buttocks finally registered in her love-hazed mind. Had she done that? Oh, God, yes. What had possessed her?

Leon, her convenient husband.

His departing words replayed in her head, and she came down to earth with a thump.

He hadn't sounded very flattered, and 'enjoyed your first taste of sex' was not how Helen would have described the act. The very word 'act' offended her sensibilities, and in that moment with sickening clarity she realised what an idiot she had been. The most emotional, momentous experience in her life had meant little to Leon. It had been just that, an *act* on his part. A way to ensure the absolute legality of their marriage, he had told her so.

For a while she had allowed herself to forget he was a hard, cynical banker, a man who controlled vast amounts of money, a man born to take account of every eventuality to control everything, Nicholas and herself included.

She cringed at her own naivety, at her own wholehearted surrender to the man. His reference to her natural ability filled her with shame and humiliation. How could she have responded to him so shockingly?

The answer was in every pore of her body, the swollen fullness of her lips and in the tender tips of her breasts, because she wanted Leon in the most primitive way possible, but had never recognised the fact.

Instinctively her awareness of him had scared her from the

very first time she had set eyes on him. She had told herself when they had met again it was silly to be afraid of the man. First impressions were usually correct, she should have remembered that, and run as far and fast as she could when he'd reappeared in her life.

It was too late now, she had married the man, and for Nicholas' sake she was going to have to live with him, but not here in his bed. She leapt off the bed, her frantic gaze flying around the room. She had to live with him, but she did not have to sleep with him. He had said they had to consummate the marriage. My God! He had certainly done that, but she wasn't hanging around for a repeat performance.

Finally finding her nightshirt on the floor, she picked it up and pulled it over her trembling body. Nicholas' room was free, she would spend the rest of the night there, and find a room of her own in the morning. Brushing her hair from her eyes, she turned towards the door.

With all the arrogant confidence of a very self-satisfied man, Leon wrapped a towel around his hips and sauntered back into the bedroom. Not only did he have Nicholas, a true Aristides, an heir to inherit his fortune, it was a pleasurable bonus to have the lovely Helen as his wife. He looked at the bed, the empty bed, and his pleasure turned to cold anger in an instant.

He glanced across the room. She was almost at the door, her glorious hair falling in a tumbled mass of waves halfway down her slender back. 'Going somewhere?' he demanded, striding towards her, and he saw her shoulders stiffen as she slowly turned to face him. Her violet eyes that had looked at him with such awe not long ago now sparkled with defiance.

'Yes, I am going to find a room of my own.'

'This is your room,' he stated angrily, not appreciating her rebellion. She had to know her place was in his bed, and he reached for her shoulders, his eyes raking over her. The cotton shirt was shapeless and ended mid calf. But it was the pattern that really caught his attention and diffused his anger somewhat. For a man accustomed to his ladies dressed in the finest silks and satins it was a real shock.

'What on earth are you wearing?' he asked incredulously. Two ridiculous teddy bears danced across her chest.

Helen hoped it was the picture holding his attention and not her breasts, but much to her shame she could do nothing about the sudden swelling in those same breasts. Leon with a slip of a towel slung around his lean hips was a breath-taking sight to any female between the ages of eight and eighty, she thought, and much to her chagrin she was no exception.

'It's my doubly-cuddly nightshirt,' she blurted. The air between them was fraught with tension and she dragged in a slightly unsteady breath before continuing. 'Nicholas likes it, he named it, and anyway it has nothing to do with you what I wear.'

'Maybe not, though your exquisite body deserves the finest silk and satin,' he opined as his hands tightened on her shoulders and he drew her closer, his dark eyes gleaming with such blatant sexuality it made her heart leap in her breast. 'But it has everything to do with me where you sleep, and that is in my bed.'

She lowered her lashes over her too-revealing eyes. She could barely look at him without blushing. 'No, thank you,' she said with all the cool she could muster. 'I want my own room.'

An amused smile played around his firm mouth. 'So polite, but that is not possible, Helen, and anyway all your clothes are here. Surely you would not want to upset Anna by demanding she move them from our suite after one night,' he prompted mockingly.

She didn't appreciate the mention of Anna or his amusement. She glanced at the rumpled bed. Obviously what had just happened there was one big laugh to him, whereas to her it was the scene of her downfall and totally humiliating.

'There is no "our" suite,' she snapped. He was so damned arrogant, nothing dented his massive male ego, and she continued defiantly, 'I'll apologise to Anna for the inconvenience tomorrow, but I am not staying here with you.'

'You don't have a choice.' His mouth tightened, his great body tensed, and all trace of humour vanished. 'You're my wife and your place is in my bed.' His eyes narrowed on her flushed, mutinous face. 'Don't try my patience. I have told you before, I don't like women who play games.'

Her face grew hot with renewed humiliation and fury. 'I am not playing a game,' she lashed back. 'You said we had to consummate the marriage—well, we have. And I have no desire to repeat the exercise.'

One eyebrow rose with derisive scorn. 'Oh, but you do.' And a hand left one shoulder to curve around her waist and draw her hard against him. 'And if you were honest you would admit that it is that desire that has you running scared.'

The contact with his big muscular body sent the blood pounding through Helen's veins. She looked up at his ruggedly attractive face. His dark eyes held a wealth of intimate, sensual knowledge that shamed and excited her, but also infuriated her beyond words.

'No,' she cried. 'I hated it. I hate you,' she flung angrily and twisted furiously against his steel-like grip, but to no avail.

His lips twisted in a humourless smile. 'You don't know me well enough to hate me. That may come later—one never knows with women,' he said dryly, his hand snaking up her back, pressing her to him from chest to thigh. 'But what you hate now is the fact that it was I who showed you what a rampant little sensualist you are, and you hate yourself for enjoying sex with someone you don't know very well.'

Her eyes glittered with angry resentment. 'That is not true; you deceived me—you behaved like an animal.'

'A male animal you thoroughly enjoyed and I have the marks to prove it,' he stated with undisguised satisfaction.

Helen blushed scarlet and lowered her lashes to disguise her vulnerability from his discerning gaze. But she could not refute it.

Lifting a hand, he cupped her chin. 'Don't let it bother you, Helen, I enjoyed receiving every one. I enjoyed you.' His thumb brushed her jaw line and the fullness of her bottom lip. 'Your problem is you enjoyed me but do not want to admit the fact.'

'No.' Her eyes glittered in angry rejection. 'I was shocked—you caught me by surprise.' And his husky chuckle did nothing for her overstretched nerves. The musky male scent of him tantalised her and the pressure of his hard body against her own overheated flesh made her tremble.

'You certainly surprised me. I could never have imagined a beautiful woman of your age would still be a virgin. Which leads me to believe that rather naively you have been labouring under the popular female illusion that some day you would fall in love and live happily ever after? Tonight was your first time and, while your body wantonly delighted in the experience, your untried emotions received a shock perfectly natural under the circumstances. I'll give you that.' His hand burrowed through her hair and he tilted her head up to his. 'You made the discovery that love, not that I believe it exists,' he drawled with cynical humour, 'is not a prerequisite for great sex, and your childish illusions are shattered.'

Her eyes blazed angrily. 'At least I had some, but you are an unfeeling, insensitive oaf.' That he was right about her did not make her feel any better, but the fact he didn't believe in love did not surprise her at all.

'Insensitive maybe, unfeeling never,' he drawled. His hand

stroked caressingly down her spine to press her into the hard strength of his thighs, so she could be in no doubt of exactly how he *felt*.

'As for taking you by surprise—' his smile was decidedly feral as he tilted her head back '—well, this time, my sweet wife, I am giving you fair warning. I am going to kiss you.'

Dark eyes merciless in their intent burned into hers. Helen wanted to look away, to break the spellbinding power of his sexuality. 'No, please.' But as his arm tightened around her all her traitorous body wanted was to surrender once again to the powerful virile strength of his.

She made a weak attempt to struggle free. But his dark head bent and his mouth covered hers, his tongue delving between her parted lips with a devastatingly skilful passion that plunged her straight back into the same state of sensual overload as before.

Her arms of their own volition wrapped around his neck. Her fingers sought the thickness of his hair, raking her fingers through its silken length with sensuous delight. She fell into his kiss like a starving woman, oblivious to everything except the man holding her, kissing her. Spinning in a whirlpool of pure pleasure over which she had no control.

'Is that please yes?' Leon husked against her mouth, sweeping her up in his arms.

Helen groaned her agreement. The first time she had felt fear, but not now. Now she was burning up with a hunger she knew only Leon could satisfy.

And when he laid her down on the bed her glittering eyes were bold as they roamed over his magnificent body. Bronzed and sleek-muscled, his skin gleamed satin in the soft light, and when she looked into his eyes the molten desire in the inky depths blinded her to everything in the world but him.

Leon stared down at her, fighting with his conscience, but

her soft, pouting mouth, her wide, inviting eyes, and the firm outline of her rigid nipples against the cotton were too tempting to resist. In one deft move he removed her shirt and gathered her into his arms, his hands moving urgently over her silken flesh. He bent his head to kiss and lick each taut nipple before returning to take her mouth with his own.

Eventually taking everything.

CHAPTER SEVEN

HELEN LAY CURLED up in a ball in the big bed, as far away from her indomitable husband as she could get. The even sound of Leon's breathing told her he was deeply asleep.

But sleep would not come for Helen; shame and humiliation burnt through her aching body at the thought of what she had allowed to happen.

How could she have been so weak willed? How could she have been so wanton? Kissing, touching, scratching.

How could her body have betrayed her so totally, not once, but twice?

Quite easily, she groaned the answer and buried her head in the pillow. She had been seduced by an expert.

The first time she had been swept away in a torrent of undreamed of pleasure as he had kissed and tasted every inch of her. Sweeping away all her virginal fears with a skill and mastery that had overwhelmed her. And when he had finally surged inside her the fierce pain had been obliterated in moments by stroke after stroke of ever-growing torturous pleasure. She had clung to him greedily, her legs locked around his waist as with all his power he had possessed her utterly, the hard strength of him filling and pulsing inside her. Until mindlessly she had cried out as her body convulsed around him in an explosion of emotion so extreme the boundaries of her self were absorbed by his.

Squirming, Helen tried to blank the memory of her second spectacular downfall from her mind. If anything her behaviour had been even worse. Boldly she had caressed and touched him, exploring him with the same intimate detail he had devoted to her. Until finally all that mattered had been the two throbbing, sweat-slicked bodies, touching, tasting, in an orgy of ever-increasing wild abandon that had culminated in a mutually explosive climax.

She heard Leon groan, and tensed, her fingers digging into the edge of the mattress. She didn't want him to wake up.

Because, painful as it was for her to admit it, for some inexplicable reason she was fast becoming incapable of resisting the man, and it could not go on. She was wise enough to know that way lay only heartache. Leon Aristides was the most autocratic, cynical man she had ever met, verging on misogynistic if his comments on the female sex were to be believed, and certainly not the sort of man to fall in love with.

Closing her eyes tight, she silently vowed to herself she would never let her arrogant husband touch her again. Tomorrow she was going to speak to Anna, and have her own room whatever Leon said, and on that thought she fell into an exhausted sleep.

Helen blinked and yawned widely, the distant sound of a door closing echoing in her head. She rolled over onto her back, and stretched, her body aching in unfamiliar places. Then she remembered, her eyes flew wide open and for a moment the sunlight streaming into the room dazzled her.

'Good morning, madam.'

Blinking again, her eyes focused on Anna standing by the bed, a laden breakfast tray in her hands,

'The master said to let you rest, but it is almost twelve and I thought you might like coffee and a little snack.'

'Twelve?' Helen squeaked and sat up in bed, her eyes straying to the indentation on the pillows next to hers. He had gone, thank heaven. Then suddenly realising she was naked, she grasped the coverlet and pulled it up under her arms, before turning a scarlet face to Anna again. 'I am sorry for oversleeping and thank you, Anna.' She took the tray from her outstretched arms. 'I certainly need something,' she muttered under her breath. 'Like a brain transplant.'

'Now, madam, no need to hurry, the master has gone to collect Nicholas and they won't be back for a while. You take your time, pamper yourself.' Anna surprised Helen by smiling broadly at her.

'And may I say, madam, I have known Master Leon since he was an eight year old, and I was first employed as his nanny. I have watched him grow into the man he is today, and I can honestly say I have never seen him look happier than he was this morning. For that I thank you. The man deserves a little happiness in his life. His mother was a difficult woman and rarely cared for him and as for his first wife…' Anna frowned. 'Still, I suppose you already know all about her and I should not waste your time gossiping. But anything you want you only have to ask.' And with another smile she left.

I wonder if that includes a separate bedroom, Helen mused darkly as she drank the coffee and ate the dainty little pastries provided. Somehow she thought not.

Her worried gaze strayed to the other side of the rumpled bed, and she was vividly reminded of last night, reminded of Leon's great golden body over her, in her, taking her yet again as the light of dawn filled the room. And placing the tray on the bedside table, she jumped out of bed and headed for the bathroom.

She turned on the shower and stood beneath the soothing

spray, trying to wash the haunting memories of last night from her mind, and determined to avoid any repeat.

Thirty minutes later with her hair dried she studied her own reflection in the mirrored wall. She looked different; her lips were still slightly swollen from Leon's kisses. Red blotches marred the pale skin of her breasts and lower over her stomach, testimony to her husband's passion.

She spun away from the mirror and quickly dressed. She didn't want to think about his passion; she didn't want to think about him, full stop. Donning a pair of blue jeans and a crisp lemon shirt, she brushed her hair back. She slipped her feet into soft flats, and ventured out of the bedroom.

Rather gingerly Helen walked down the marble staircase. She was sore in a way and in places she had never been before and it was all Leon's fault.

And there he was standing at the bottom of the stairs like a replay of yesterday, only this time he was casually dressed in a cream wool sweater and dark trousers and Nicholas was at his side rather than hers.

'Uncle Leon said we had to let you rest,' Nicholas chirped up, and Helen turned scarlet and her new husband smiled, and today the smile did reach his knowing eyes, and made her blush even more.

'Yes, well,' Helen murmured, reaching the bottom of the stairs and giving Nicholas a big hug. 'Now tell me all about your night away.'

Nicholas duly obliged while Anna served lunch and Helen's tension eased somewhat. Afterwards Leon, much to her surprise, insisted on taking Nicholas upstairs for his nap and promised to play football with the boy later, while Anna gave Helen a guided tour of the house.

The eight bedrooms and five reception rooms impressed Helen but she could not help thinking it was a bit soulless.

Immaculate with high ornate ceilings, brilliant frescos and marble floors, and the furniture to match it was perfect. A little too perfect, a typical stiff-necked banker's abode.

But she did take the opportunity to confide in Anna that she was an illustrator and ask her if she could have a room for a study, preferably not too far from Nicholas' room, because she usually worked when he was asleep. Anna quite happily obliged and showed her to a bedroom, along the corridor from Nicholas'. When Anna went downstairs Helen swiftly unpacked her portable easel and sketch books and removed some essential items of clothing from the master suite. She didn't care what Leon thought. She was having her own room.

Surprisingly the rest of the day was quite fun. She joined Nicholas and Leon in the garden; after yesterday's rain it was pleasant to be outdoors in the sunshine. She was cajoled into playing a game of football, and burst out laughing when her usually imposing husband fell over the ball in his haste to take it off her and sprawled at her feet. Nicholas immediately jumped on his back and demanded he pretend to be a horse and give him a ride.

There was something very satisfying in seeing Leon on his knees. 'Ride him, cowboy,' Helen shouted encouragement.

But when Nicholas tired of the game, Leon slanted a wicked look up at her.

'Your turn, Helen,' and glancing at Nicholas he added, 'What do you think—should I give Helen a ride?'

'Yes. Yes,' Nicholas shouted, his little face wreathed in smiles.

'No, you should not,' Helen declared, blushing scarlet at the sexual connotation that flew right over the child's head. But she was secretly pleased at how well they all got along. Leon looked almost boyish and more relaxed than she had ever seen him when Nicholas was around, which was a good sign for the family she hoped they could eventually become.

Turning her back on the laughing duo, she flung over her shoulder, 'And now I think it is time for tea.'

'Sorry, Nicholas, Helen thinks she is too old to play.'

She heard his mocking comment and spun back round to find him grinning down at her.

'Old, *moi?*'she exclaimed, her violet eyes sparkling with humour. 'You have some nerve at your age.' She saw his dark eyes flash a warning, and, turning, she sprinted for the house with both Nicholas and Leon chasing her.

Bath time was a joint venture and when Nicholas was finally in bed Leon left to return some business calls and Helen stayed to read him a story.

When she walked into the dining room two hours later, Helen immediately sensed the easygoing atmosphere of the afternoon had gone. If it had ever existed except in her mind. Leon wearing a black shirt with a button down collar and black trousers, was standing by the drinks cabinet, a glass in his hand, a brooding expression on his hard face. Casually dressed, he looked incredibly attractive and nothing like a banker, more of a bandit, Helen thought fancifully.

She frowned. His shirt was probably tailor-made by Turnbull and Asser and his trousers similarly designer-labelled. He could afford the best that money could buy, so why wouldn't he look amazing? she told herself, determined to deny her growing attraction for the man.

Leon saw her frown, his own expression one of cool indifference, but inside he was anything but indifferent. For a man who prided himself on his rigid self-discipline it was disturbing to realise he had absolutely no control over the instant reaction of his body. Not since he was a teenager had he felt anything so urgent, if then, and it bothered him.

She was wearing a soft blue wraparound dress that emphasised her tiny waist and moulded her hips and thighs like a second skin. Her legs were covered in silk stockings and on her feet she was wearing high-heeled navy shoes. Her long fair hair was piled up on top of her head in a loose knot, a few stray tendrils framing her small face. She looked exquisite and elegant and she had surprised him again.

The wedding dress yesterday and now this, his image of her, first as a young Lolita, devious and money-hungry, and then as an earth-mother type in jeans and sweater, was constantly changing and it worried him.

He was a man renowned for his brilliant analytical brain, a man without emotion who made decisions in the realms of big business on a daily basis with an absolute conviction that was always successful. So why could he not read his own wife so easily?

'Would you like a drink?' he demanded curtly.

'No, thanks. I'll have a glass of wine with dinner.' She glanced at him and sat down at the table, ignoring him.

Taking the seat opposite her, he filled their wineglasses and as Anna served the first course he watched Helen through thoughtful if frustrated eyes. She was an enigma to him. Like no other woman he had ever met. Beautiful and surprisingly innocent, caring and compassionate as was evident from watching her interaction with the boy. Then add secretive and avid little sensualist and the mixture was dynamite and dangerous to his peace of mind.

He ate the seafood starter deep in thought. He had never given the women in his life more than a passing thought outside the bedroom. But Helen troubled him, and he did not like the feeling.

As Anna removed the plates and set down the main course he thanked her and, glancing at his silent wife, he had the distinct impression she was here on sufferance, and he did not like that either. Nor was he entirely comfortable with the semi-aroused state that afflicted him every time he set eyes on her.

'Tomorrow, Helen, I am in meetings all day until the evening,' he said decisively. She was his wife and he was worrying about nothing, he decided. All he had to do was carry on as before, working all day, only now he could look forward to sating himself in her luscious little body all night.

'I have arranged for Mary Stefano to take you and Nicholas to see the nursery school I have enrolled him in. Mary's youngest children already attend and they love it.'

After eating in silence Helen was surprised when Leon spoke. She looked across the wide expanse of the formal dining table to where he sat. He was forking steak into his mouth with obvious enjoyment, completely unperturbed by her presence. Unfortunately she did not have the same luxury. The tension she always felt around him had returned in spades as soon as Nicholas was tucked up in bed asleep.

'And have I no say in the matter?' she demanded.

'In this case, no, it is done.'

'And if I don't like it?' she asked coolly, but inside she was burning with anger. He was so damned autocratic. 'I am his guardian just as much as you. You should have at least consulted me first.'

He looked over at her, a frown crossing his broad brow. 'Take my word for it, the nursery school is the best in Athens, and as the boy already knows Mary's children he will have no trouble settling in quickly.'

'Why should I?' What he said made perfect sense, but Helen was spoiling for an argument. From the minute Leon had walked into her life he had taken her over, as he did his blasted banks, with a forceful, single-minded determination it was almost impossible to fight. Resentment bubbled up inside her, as much at her own weakness as his strength, and changing tack she said bitterly, 'You railroaded me into having dinner with you rather than with Nicholas the night I arrived.' She shoved her plate away.

'Well, I don't want to do it your way. I don't like to eat late. I prefer to have a light lunch and an early supper, not huge meals twice a day, and I can't eat another thing.' She knew she was being petty but she couldn't seem to stop herself, and, reaching for her glass of wine, she took a long swallow.

'How we got from choosing schools to what time dinner is served I won't even try to discern. The female mind is a mystery to me.' His dark eyes roamed slowly over her, lingering on the shadowed cleavage displayed by the neckline of her dress, before he raised his gaze to capture hers. Something flashed in his eyes that looked like amusement.

'But in case you had not noticed I am a large man, Helen. A cheese sandwich and scrambled eggs on toast and a bit of bacon does not come anywhere near to satisfying me for a day.' His dark eyes gleamed with rueful amusement. 'Though I can see how it would satisfy Nicholas and someone of your stature.'

She resented the dig about her size—though she hadn't minded the *ma petite* when he made love to her, the treacherous thought popped into her head. Then Helen recalled serving him just the food he had mentioned the day he had turned up at her house and she was mortified and angry at the reminder, a telling tide of pink washing over her pale cheeks.

'You should have said at the time if you were still hungry. You are certainly not shy of saying exactly what you want in every other respect,' she declared bluntly.

'True.' He chuckled. 'But as soon as I reached the hotel I ordered room service, so don't beat yourself up about it.'

She saw the humour in his dark eyes and was infuriated. 'As if I ever would over you,' she snorted. She might have guessed Leon was not the type of man to do without anything he wanted.

'Stranger things have happened,' Leon remarked. Her violet eyes were bright as sapphires against her flushed skin, the blue dress folded low between her pert breasts revealing the blush covered more than her face and was not solely with anger, and his body responded accordingly.

'You never know—one day when you get to know me a little better you might feel differently. But in the meantime finish your meal. I don't want you weak with hunger for what I have in mind.'

His taunting, none-too-subtle innuendo was the last straw for Helen. 'I have finished,' she shot back, flashing him a furious glance. The dark eyes that met hers gleamed with a sensuality she could not help but recognise. Her heart raced and her mouth went dry and she hated her own weakness. Leaping to her feet, she pushed back her chair. 'I am going to check on Nicholas—after all, that is the only reason I'm here.'

'As you say.' He cast a knowing look up at her, before glancing down at the watch on his wrist and then back to her flushed face. 'I have a few calls to make to the Far East. I will be up in an hour or two.' And with a dismissive nod of his dark head he returned to his steak.

Helen hoped it choked him, and slammed the door behind her as she left.

She looked around the huge reception hall and sighed. She had probably overreacted slamming the door, but she didn't care. She stopped by the kitchen and told Anna she had had enough to eat and was going to bed with a mug of cocoa, much to Anna's disgust.

She made her way upstairs, and, ignoring the master suite, she glanced in on Nicholas, and then continued along the hall to the room at the end. Closing the door behind her, she quickly undressed and then had a quick wash in the small *en suite* and, slipping on a plain white nightshirt she crawled into the queen-sized bed.

Settling back against the pillows, she cast a satisfied glance around the room and took a sip of her cocoa. It was much smaller than the master suite, but it had a small bathroom and was subtly decorated in cream and buttercup yellow. Along one wall was a chest of drawers, dressing table and a wardrobe. A sofa and chair and small table had been arranged by the window, but she had pushed them to one side and set up her portable easel and placed her sketch books, pencils, pastels and paints on the foot-deep window sill. It wasn't perfect, but the light was good and it would do, she thought complacently.

She eased back against the headboard and took another sip of hot chocolate feeling calmer than she had done since the moment she had set foot in Greece two days ago. She had to accept this was her life now if she wanted to stay with Nicholas, and she did. She loved him to distraction; he was the only child she would ever have and it would kill her to be parted from him.

As for her hard-headed husband, surely he would see the sense in keeping their relationship one of friendship rather than sex. From her very limited experience sex simply caused unwanted tensions in a relationship, which could not be good for Nicholas.

After all, he was the only reason for their marriage. She was under no illusion that Leon cared for her. She was probably a novelty to him, an inexperienced little innocent that happened to live in his house. He was a man of the world who could take his pick of beautiful women. It would be no hardship for him to find someone else to sate his overactive libido with. For all Helen knew he probably had a mistress or two waiting for him somewhere.

Why her heart sank at the thought she didn't want to examine too closely, and sipped some more cocoa.

CHAPTER EIGHT

THE SUDDEN CLICK of a door opening made Helen's heart skip a beat and she looked warily across the room. Fury rippled through her as she saw Leon's tall frame outlined in the opening and unconsciously she pulled the cover up higher.

'What do you want?' she demanded and silently cursed her choice of words as one dark brow arched eloquently in her direction. But defiantly she held his gaze as he walked towards her.

'Now that is a leading question if ever I heard one,' he drawled, and stopped by the side of the bed. 'And one I am sure you can answer if you care to try,' he prompted silkily.

Leon's hard black eyes swept over his errant wife. He noted her scarlet face framed by the silken mass of her ash-blonde hair tumbling over her shoulders, the prim cotton nightshirt skimming over her firm breasts, and he wanted to strangle her.

How dared the little witch try to defy him again? Last night he had taken her innocence with perhaps not as much finesse as he would have liked. But after the initial shock she had been with him all the way and later he could have sworn he had calmed any virginal fears that still lingered. He had the marks to prove it, so what the hell was her game? A cold, disdainful smile twisted his wide mouth. He had had more than enough with his first wife trying to tie him in knots with sex. He had soon disillusioned her and he was damned if he was going to let this one try the same tricks.

With each passing second Helen was conscious of the building tension. She could feel his barely leashed anger almost physically, but she refused to respond to his suggestive jibe. Instead she simply stared up at him. Her heart was pounding in her chest, her conviction of moments ago that Leon would see reason taking a nosedive. And what had happened to the calls he was supposed to be making? He'd said hours and it was barely thirty minutes.

'Nothing to say, Helen?' His black eyes, cold and hard as stone, stared down into hers.

'You said you were going to work,' she snapped back and tried to ignore the trickle of fear snaking its way down her spine.

'So I did, but Anna, while berating me on allowing my very new bride to go to bed on her own, also let slip that you had chosen a bedroom for a study.' His hard mouth twisted in a derisive smile. 'She is a trusting soul and I doubt it ever crossed her mind you would sleep in the room. But, surprise, surprise, I am nowhere near as trusting and decided to check.'

'Oh.'

'*Oh.*' His dark eyes mocked her ruthlessly. 'Is that all you have to say for yourself?'

Helen swallowed down the nervous lump in her throat and said bravely, 'I told you last night I was not sharing your room again.'

'Why?' he demanded with an arrogance that maddened her. 'After last night there is not a part of your body that I don't know intimately.'

It was true. But it did not help her precarious hold on her temper to be reminded and she dragged an angry breath into her oxygen-starved lungs. 'You are disgusting,' she spat, and tore her gaze away from his harshly attractive face.

Leon moved closer, his big body looming over her intimidatingly. His black shirt was pulled taut across his broad shoulders, the top three buttons were undone, revealing his black curling body hair. At least he had not undressed, she thought, a sudden shameful image of him naked flashing through her mind. 'Go away.' And she meant from her mind as much as the room. 'Just go away.'

Without a word he reached down and wrenched the covers from her grasp.

'Don't you dare,' she cried, grabbing the cover with her free hand before flinging the mug of cocoa straight at him.

The mug bounced off his chest, spreading hot chocolate all over him. She saw his head jerk back and she stared in absolute horror at what she had done. Usually she was the calmest, most even-tempered of women. She had never committed a violent act in her life. Oh, my God! She might have scalded him; a little higher, she could have scarred his face.

'I'm sorry, so sorry,' she said, her guilt ridden gaze fixed on his.

Leon's face was as black as thunder, his dark eyes hard as jet. 'You damn well will be.'

He swore and hauled her out of the bed, throwing her over his shoulder. She tried to struggle, suddenly very afraid, but he was far too powerful for her. He stormed straight into the bathroom and, dropping her to the floor, he locked the door behind him.

Dizzy from being held upside down, the blood pounding in her head, she took a moment to focus. When she did she saw he had removed his shirt and his chest hair was damp and sticky with cocoa.

'I really am sorry.' She tried to apologise, but she was too late.

He gave her a killing look. His arm clamped around her waist, and, kicking off his shoes, he herded her into the shower.

He turned on the water, and spun her around to face him. He grasped her hand and slapped the soap in her palm. 'Now you are going to wash off every drop of your crazy handiwork,' he hissed with a sibilant softness that was more frightening than his anger.

The water pounded down on her, and she stared at him wide-eyed and terrified. He was only inches away from her and she did not need her contact lenses to see every muscle and sinew in his great body was taut with rage. For once she thanked the Lord she was small. Her head barely reached his shoulders and she did not have to look at his hard, furious face. But her embarrassment was acute as the water plastered her shirt to her skin revealing every curve and hollow of her body.

'What are you waiting for?' His hands caught her wrist and lifted her hand to his chest. 'Wash.'

She swallowed down the refusal that sprang to her lips, and began lathering his chest. The feel of his warm, wet skin beneath her palm, the hard musculature of his chest, were a sensual torture that made her heart race.

'Use both hands. I am a big man,' he ordered harshly.

She closed her eyes and, rubbing the soap between her palms, she splayed her hands on his chest and moved them in ever-widening circles. He felt so good and, appalled at where her thoughts were taking her she gasped.

'There.' Her eyes flying open, she moved back until the wall of the shower stopped her. 'It is done.'

Drenched and battling to keep his rage under control, Leon stared furiously down at her. She was done when he said so. He caught the shimmer of sexual awareness in the darkening depths of her violet eyes. Saw her small, perfectly formed breasts peaking against the wet shirt and suddenly, from being rigid with fury at her wild action, he felt his body hardening with a totally different emotion.

'Not yet, it isn't,' he told her. 'Not to my satisfaction.'

Shedding his trousers, he reached for her and stripped the shirt from her body.

'No,' she tried to object.

But her denial was weak. Triumph surged though him along with a devilish desire to possess her so completely and utterly that she would never again try to defy him. Sliding an arm around her back he drew her against him.

'Yes, Helen,' he drawled and, taking her chin between his fingers and thumb, he forced her to look at him.

'The chocolate flowed down my body. You need to wash lower,' he commanded silkily, stroking a hand up her back before trailing down the indentation of her spine to finally curve her pert rear. For a moment he felt her slight resistance. He pressed her closer against his now throbbing arousal and felt her shudder in helpless response.

Wet, naked and held against his big body, Helen was vitally aware of the hard strength of him against her belly. She stared up at him and the mocking eyes that held hers gleamed with a molten sensuality that made her stomach somersault. With her whole body reacting treacherously to the sliding caress of his hand against her naked flesh, she could barely breathe. Desire lanced through her, weakening her resistance, still she tried to shake her head free from his hold. But his grip tightened on her chin.

'Every action has a reaction. Remember that, Helen, and we will get along fine.' He moved his hand from her chin to sweep the wet hair from her face.

'But I'll spare your blushes this time,' he declared softly his dark eyes gleaming with an unholy light. Taking the soap from her unresisting hand he stroked it down his chest and lower between their bodies.

She was pressed against the impressive length of him, and the back of his hand trailing down her quivering stomach ignited a burning desire in her trembling body that shook her to the depths of her being. She did not want to feel this way about him. Then, turning his hand, he cupped her between her thighs and it was so shockingly intimate Helen couldn't hold back a moan.

He gave a low laugh and proceeded to lather her there, everywhere. She closed her eyes as he explored and caressed her hot, wet flesh, all thought of resistance banished from her mind. She shuddered as his hand stroked back up over her stomach and on to massage the fullness of her breasts. When he had dropped the soap she had no idea. The water blinded her and her whole body pulsed with pleasure.

'I am almost done,' he said roughly. 'You really do have the most delectable body.'

A helpless moan escaped her and she reached for his broad shoulders. His dark head bent and he urged her against the strong power of his thighs as his mouth took savage possession of hers. Her head was impelled back against the shower wall at the force of his kiss, but she didn't notice as she shook with need and responded with a blind hunger of her own.

His tongue explored her mouth with a white-hot sexual force that drove her out of her mind. When he lifted her, his strong hands cupping her buttocks, she instinctively crossed her legs around his waist, frantic for him to fill her, possess her, wanting him with a passion that was almost pain.

He looked at her, his dark eyes glittering with a primitive pagan light as he thrust into her hard and deep.

She cried out, her body moving instinctively in the fast and furious rhythm he set. His mouth sought her breast and dragged hungrily on the straining nipple as he plunged harder and faster until she thought she would die from the pleasure. She dug her fingers in his neck. She felt her whole body lock in incredible tension, then shatter into excruciatingly exquisite spasms that went on and on. She dimly heard the animal growl as his great body bucked and shuddered violently, his seed spilling inside her as he joined her in an explosive climax. She buried her head in the curve of his neck as the seemingly endless tremors very slowly receded.

'Helen, are you okay?'

Helen heard the question and lifted her head. He was watching her from beneath heavy-lidded eyes, waiting for an answer, and suddenly she was terribly self-conscious. Wrapped around him like a clinging vine, she felt the reality of the situation hit her. But her own innate honesty would not let her deny her response to him, he only had to touch her and she melted like ice on a fire.

'I'm fine,' she murmured.

It was the answer Leon wanted and slowly he lowered her to her feet. He turned off the water and cupped her head in his hands and gently swept back the tangled mass of her hair from her face before placing a soft kiss on her lush lips.

'Good. Me too,' he admitted huskily. 'So no more arguments about sharing my bed, hmm.' He lifted her out of the shower and, taking a towel from the rail, he wrapped it around her back.

She was everything he remembered from the very first time he'd set eyes on her years ago. Her breasts were high and firm with perfect pink tips, her waist tiny, and now he knew she was a natural blonde. She was so much more than he had expected. From the very beginning he had sensed her awareness of him, known he could have her, but he had never imagined she would be so wildly responsive to him.

'And no more flinging cups of chocolate.' He knotted the

towel between her breasts and stepped back. 'I am not easy to anger, but I do have a temper,' he admitted and, taking another towel, he wrapped it around his hips.

Helen gazed at him helplessly. He was so cool, so in control it was incredible, whereas she did not know herself any more, her emotions were all over the place. Honesty forced her to admit it was her temper that had started the confrontation and his temper that had got them in here. As for what had happened afterwards, it was as much her fault as his, she thought, glancing around the small, steamy room.

'Oh, my God! I can't believe I did that in a bathroom.' Not realising she was speaking the thought out loud.

'I won't tell anyone if you don't,' Leon mocked, his lips parting in a broad grin, his dark eyes sparkling with amusement colliding with hers.

'Hardly,' she cried, shocked, but his humour and his grin were irresistible and her own lips quirked at the corners in a reciprocating smile. 'I wasn't thinking.' And she was fast losing her mind again; Leon looking relaxed and happy was a seductive sight.

'Let me do the thinking for both of us, and in future I think we should stick to our bedroom,' he declared, swinging her up in his arms. 'That way we will have a long and contented marriage.'

'That is the most chauvinistic comment I have ever heard,' Helen stated. 'And will you stop sweeping me off my feet all the time? I can walk,' she almost wailed.

Held in his arms she felt helpless and vulnerable and a whole host of emotions she did not want to face. So much for her vow never to let him touch her again.

'I love the way you walk, but it is so much quicker carrying you to bed,' he said with a wicked grin, carrying her out of the bathroom.

'Please put me down. I need to pick up my clothes.' She glanced around the room and began to struggle. 'Anna will be horrified at the mess we have made.'

'You worry too much,' he mocked. 'Anna won't mind; she has plenty of staff to help her clean up.'

He glanced around the room, and paused. He had been too angry to notice the room when he had stormed in, his whole attention on the woman in the bed, but now he looked around. Some furniture was shoved against one wall, and an easel stood in front of the window with books, paints and other stuff littering the deep window sill.

'You paint,' he said in astonishment, and some memory niggled at the back of his mind. 'Why didn't you tell me?'

'I'm an illustrator,' she snapped, wriggling in his arms. 'I thought it was obvious. I told you my wedding dress was Nicholas' choice. It was the same style as the one the fairy is wearing in the picture on his bedroom wall at home, the one I did for a children's book. I am not the useless little woman you seem to think, and will you put me down?'

Leon's eyes flared. Of course, the drawing in the boy's room. He looked down into her flushed face with barely concealed amusement in his. That was why he had thought she looked familiar on their wedding day, her dress had been a replica of the one the fairy wore, he realised, though on Helen it had looked sexy, but, yes, a little fey.

'I didn't believe you when you said Nicholas had chosen your dress.' He shook his head in wonder. His wife was a talented artist along with her more obvious talents. She never ceased to surprise him.

He tightened his hold on her and pressed a swift kiss on top of her head. 'You and I need to talk. I want to know what other secrets you are keeping from me. But not here.' He strode forward.

She glanced around the messy bedroom as he headed for the door and for some reason she felt as if she owed him an explanation. 'I asked Anna for a room for a studio. She didn't know I was going to sleep here.'

'I am sure she didn't,' Leon drawled, striding into the hall. 'Anna is a hopeless romantic and I see no reason to disillusion her.' He glanced down at her flushed face. 'Luckily you and I have no such illusions, correct?'

'I am not sure I know what you mean,' Helen murmured as he elbowed the door open into the master suite and gently lowered her to her feet, his hands loosely clasping her waist.

His dark eyes narrowed astutely on her guarded face. 'Anna has romantic notions of love and marriage out of all proportion to reality. Probably because she has never married,' he said cynically. 'Take it from one who knows: what you and I have is so much better.'

'And what exactly do we have?' Helen asked, her heart sinking. The passionate lover of moments ago, the man who had awakened her body in a way she had never dreamt possible, was once again looking at her with cold, mocking eyes. And it crossed her mind to wonder why he was so hard-hearted, or if he had a heart at all.

'We have a child to care for, and we have this.' As his mouth took hers in a kiss that left her lips tingling and her temper rising.

'Sex,' she spat.

'Don't be so quick to knock it, Helen. Great sex is a hell of a lot more than some so-called love matches ever achieve,' he stated decisively.

'And however much your conservative little mind wishes it was otherwise, the physical chemistry between us is dynamite.'

For her, yes, but for Leon she wasn't so sure. He was a sophisticated, experienced lover and he had not got that way being celibate, she thought bitterly.

'I have to take your word for that as I have no experience except you to draw on. According to Delia, not something the Aristides men ever suffer from much past puberty. They are noted for their obedient wives and countless mistresses,' she drawled derisively.

'Damn Delia,' he swore. 'She got an idea in her head and stuck with it to the end, just like our mother.'

'Your mother?' she queried, momentarily diverted from her seething resentment of the man.

His mouth twisted in a cold smile. 'Your interest in my family has been long but flawed, sweetheart. Maybe it is time you heard the truth.' Leading her to the bed, he sat down and pulled her down beside him, a long arm sliding around her waist to keep her there.

'You and I need to have a talk to get a few things straight. As you said I was labouring under the illusion you did nothing except look after children, and now I know different. You're an artist in your own right. Tomorrow a proper studio will be provided for you. But by the same token your concept of me is totally coloured by Delia's opinions of her family and not necessarily true.'

'Says you,' she snorted.

He ignored her jibe and continued, 'Contrary to what you think, my father never blamed Delia for our mother's suicide. If anyone was to blame it was probably me.'

'You?' His statement surprised and intrigued her.

'Yes. After I was born she had a mental breakdown.' A wry smile twisted his hard mouth at her shocked expression. 'She was in and out of hospital for years. Why do you think there was a fifteen-year gap between Delia and I?'

Not waiting for her response he continued. 'My father

worshipped her. At that time postnatal depression was a relatively new concept and was suggested by the top consultant my father had hired to treat her. My father believed the diagnosis and was determined not to get her pregnant again, although later the consultant diagnosed bipolar disorder as well.' He threw out his hands. 'But mistakes happen. As for him having a mistress—he never looked at another woman until long after mother had died.'

'But Delia...' she began, and stopped as she realised Anna's comment earlier today that his mother never cared for him gave credence to Leon's explanation. And it went a long way to explain his hard, emotionless attitude towards women. It was hardly surprising for a young boy who was never shown love by his mother to grow up not believing in the concept.

'Listen for a moment,' Leon said curtly. 'Hard as it is for me to admit, with hindsight I think maybe Delia was heading for the same problem.'

'You really think that?' Helen exclaimed.

'Yes.' He nodded with a grim look about his firm mouth. 'Did it never occur to you that Delia gave her baby into your care remarkably easily? And from what I can gather she wasn't around very much.'

'No, certainly not,' Helen shot back. She didn't want to think Delia could have been wrong in her assessment of her own family, because if she did it made her own actions indefensible. 'She asked me to care for Nicholas before he was born. She told me—'

'I know what she told you,' he cut her off. 'And you're probably right—forget I said anything and let's get back to us.'

For Leon to agree with her was a shock to her system, and paradoxically not one she could fully accept, but what happened next was an even bigger shock.

He placed his hand on her cheek and tilted her head

towards him. 'As for me—' his dark eyes locked on hers with piercing intensity '—I am older than you, and naturally there have been a number of women in my life. But I can assure you I have always been monogamous for as long as a relationship lasted, and I was never unfaithful to my wife as long as she was faithful to me.'

'I see,' Helen murmured, quietened by the thought of his first wife. Tina had been very beautiful and had died tragically along with her baby. Maybe that was another reason why Leon did not believe in love any more. Because maybe, contrary to what Helen had been led to believe, he had loved Tina and she had been cruelly taken from him.

'Do you, I wonder?' He raised his black brows over his deep-set dark eyes and caught her hand in his and lifted it to his lips, kissing the gold band on her finger. 'Ours may have been a convenient marriage, Helen, but there is no reason why it can't be mutually beneficial. You and I have a lot more in common than you seem to think.'

That she didn't believe. 'You are joking—a wealthy world banker and a stay-at-home illustrator. I don't see the connection somehow,' she observed dryly.

'We both adore Nicholas and want what is best for him— agreed?' She nodded her head. 'We both do work we enjoy?' She nodded again. 'The sex is great, and so long as you remember I am the only man you are going to sleep with there should be no problem.'

'What about you?' Helen shot back. 'You as good as told me you could not count the number of women you have known and in true chauvinist fashion you have the nerve to demand my fidelity.'

'Yes, absolutely.' He looked at her with amusement and something else in his black eyes. 'But you can demand the same from me, and I will happily comply.'

His firm lips quirked at the corners and he smiled down at her. 'Is that what you want?'

Twenty-four hours ago she would have told him she didn't give a damn what or who he did. But now, with his hand still clasping hers, and held in the strong, protective curve of his arm with the warmth of his naked thigh pressed against her own, she knew it would be a lie.

She did care. Because right or wrong she wanted him, and the very thought of him taking another woman to his bed made her sick to her stomach.

'Yes, fidelity cuts both ways,' she said flatly and, determined not to let him know she cared, she qualified her response sanctimoniously with, 'We need to set a good example for Nicholas.'

'You're right, of course. I bow to your superior wisdom,' he drawled with mock solemnity.

'Very funny.' She tried to pull her hand from his but he tightened his grip.

'I am deadly serious, Helen. I am a hundred per cent in favour of a mutually exclusive relationship. I don't need any other woman with you in my bed. So let's call a truce. You stop resenting the fact that you enjoy sex. Relax and stop trying to fight me. And I will stop, what was it you said?' He grinned. 'I will stop sweeping you off your feet all the time. Agreed?'

His dark eyes smiled confidently into hers. The conceited devil knew he only had to look at her to figuratively sweep her off her feet, never mind physically, she thought wryly, but she could not help smiling at his audacious deal, and nodded her head in agreement.

She did not have a choice, because, whether it was just sex as Leon believed or something more as she feared, he had aroused a hunger in her, a need that she wasn't ready to give up just yet. If ever, she thought as he tipped her back on the bed.

CHAPTER NINE

HELEN STIRRED, LAZILY conscious of the warmth of a hard male body pressed against her back, and the gentle caress of a hand at her breast. Her eyes flickered open and dreamily she registered the firm lips nuzzling her neck and instinctively turned towards the source of pleasure.

Her eyes widened. 'Leon.'

His broad chest was angled towards her, a question gleaming in his dark smouldering eyes. A swift tug of desire plucked at her heart strings and she could no more deny him or herself as the events of last night flashed through her brain and, equally quickly, a blush covered her whole body.

'I should hope so, Helen,' he mocked, and his lips brushed lightly against her mouth sending a shiver through her. 'I am your husband.' He chuckled softly.

As if programmed to his touch her lips parted, her eyes drifted shut and she helplessly surrendered to the exquisite temptation of his kiss.

'What the hell?'

She groaned at the abrupt withdrawal of his mouth from hers. She heard the roar and opened her eyes to see Nicholas scrambling up over Leon's thighs towards her.

'Helen.' Chubby arms reached out to her, his little face all smiles. Immediately she raised her arms to cuddle him, but Leon sat up and took a firm hold on the boy.

'Good morning, Nicholas,' he greeted dryly, pressing a swift kiss on his small head. 'You and I, young man, have to have a talk. First rule of the house is you do not barge into our bedroom at the crack of dawn. Understand?'

'What are you doing in my Helen's bed?' Nicholas demanded.

'We are married and married couples share a bed.'

'So why can't I come in at dawn?'

Helen glanced at Leon and hid a smile. He looked so adorable with his black hair curling haphazardly over his brow, and so magnificently male. His broad, muscular chest gleamed in the morning light and the swiftly placed coverlet he had dragged over his thighs did not quite hide the embarrassing state of his sex. The perplexed, frustrated expression on his dark face said it all. He was about to discover sex was not everything in a marriage. He was being thrown into fatherhood at the deep end and he hadn't a clue, she thought, and waited to hear her very new husband's answer.

'Because Helen is my wife now, and I said so.'

What a cop-out. She watched with interest as the man and boy with almost identical eyes stared at each other, fully expecting Nicholas to yell his displeasure at being denied his early-morning cuddle.

But to her amazement he rested a hand on Leon's chest and turned his big eyes to her. 'Mark said that now you two are married that makes you my mum and dad. Is that right?'

It was Helen's turn to be lost for words. But Leon had no such problem.

'Mark is right,' he said. 'We are officially your mother and father.'

'Then I can call you Mum and Dad?'

Helen was stunned and watched as Leon simply ruffled the boy's hair with a gentle hand and smiled.

'If you want to call us Mum and Dad, that is fine.' Turning his head, he fixed dark eyes on Helen's, a challenging light in the inky depths that she could not ignore. 'Isn't it, Helen?'

She tore her gaze from his and pushed a shaky hand through her hair, sweeping it from her face, and looked at Nicholas. His big eyes were dark and softly pleading and she knew she had reached the ultimate point of no return.

She had married Leon so she could stay with Nicholas, be a mother to him, but she had not really considered Leon as anything other than his uncle. In the back of her mind she had thought a man like Leon would not want too close a commitment to another man's child—after all, he would probably want to father a child of his own one day.

He had shocked her with his instant acceptance of Nicholas' request. Some day maybe she had thought Nicholas would accept them as his mum and dad. But that it had happened so quickly surprised her. His biological mother had died only two months ago, and though she knew Delia would only ever have wanted what made Nicholas happy she could not help feeling guilty. The death of her best friend had given Helen her dearest wish and the thought played on her conscience, life seemed so unfair.

Not just because of her guilt that Nicholas had accepted her as his mum so swiftly, but also because it had suddenly occurred to her that Leon had not used any protection after the first time they had made love. If he harboured some misguided belief that she would provide him with a child he was in for a big disappointment.

She would have to tell him.

'Helen.'

She heard Leon prompt, and knew now wasn't the time.

And unless she wanted to look like a wicked witch of the west to Nicholas, she had to agree, and in her heart of hearts she knew it was what she wanted, and with a silent prayer of thanks to Delia she agreed.

'Yes, darling.' She reached for Nicholas and cuddled him against her, tears of sadness and joy stinging her eyes. 'Uncle Leon and I love you very much and we would be honoured to be called Mum and Dad, if that's what you want. But you do understand you must always remember Delia with happiness and joy as the mother who gave you life. Okay?'

'Yes, great…Mum,' he said with a grin, and hugged her back.

'Come on, Nicholas.' Leon slid off the bed, tucking a discarded towel from last night around his lean hips, much to Helen's relief, and plucked Nicholas from her arms.

'I will help you get dressed, and Helen can have a rest. She needs it.' He winked at her. 'And you need a nanny.'

'What is a nanny?' Helen heard Nicholas ask as Leon swept him up on his shoulders and headed out of the room.

His answer was lost to Helen by the closing of the door. At the same time she realised another door had closed. Leon had laid down the rules and Nicholas saw them as his mum and dad who shared a bed. Unless she was prepared to upset him, that was how it must stay. The hoary old saying that she had made her bed and now she had to lie in it sprang to mind.

And being brutally honest she was not averse to the idea any more. It had been very pleasant to wake up in Leon's arms.

That evening over dinner she was convinced she had made the right decision when Leon suggested they should legally adopt Nicholas, and make him truly their own. He reckoned it would be quite straightforward as he was the boy's uncle and she was already his guardian and he would get Chris to look into it straight away. Helen thought it was a marvellous idea. She would be Nicholas' mother, not just his guardian until he was twenty-one but legally for life, and later in bed that night she didn't think of resisting when Leon took her in his arms.

The next six weeks were a revelation for Helen. On better acquaintance with Anna, she very quickly realised her help was not needed in the well-oiled running of the house. A young girl, Marta, was hired as Nicholas' nanny, much against Helen's wishes. But Leon simply overrode her arguments, pointing out as his wife she would have social commitments to fulfil and it was unfair to expect Anna or any of the other staff to take on the extra work of babysitter. Plus, he had added with a gleam in his dark eyes, he didn't appreciate the boy crawling over him first thing in the morning, not when he was with her. Then kissed her senseless.

The one job Helen insisted on was taking Nicholas to nursery school, but as a chauffeur-driven car transported them there and back it wasn't really necessary. The high spot of her morning was meeting Mary after dropping the children off and sharing a leisurely coffee and gossip with her at a local café.

At first she had felt guilty at keeping the chauffeur waiting but Mary had quickly disabused her of the notion, telling her it was normal in Leon's world to have a car waiting at all times, and did she really want to put the driver out of a job for the dubious pleasure of driving through the chaotic Athens traffic herself? And though she was a good driver her answer was a resounding no.

Usually, after collecting Nicholas from nursery school, they had lunch together and she spent some time playing with him, before spending an hour or two on her artwork. Sometimes she left him in the nanny's care and worked some more or went on the occasional shopping trip with Mary around the expensive stores and boutiques of Athens, as she was doing today.

As for her husband, she knew him a little better now than

when they had first met and she was cautiously hopeful for the future. He appeared rather austere to most people, which she conceded was hardly surprising given he seemed to have had a pretty loveless childhood. She didn't doubt he had genuinely cared for his sister, but the age gap between them probably accounted for the misconceptions they had had of each other. Yet Leon was brilliant with Nicholas when he had the time, and when the three of them were together usually at weekends, she could almost believe they were a family.

But Leon was a difficult man to truly know except in the biblical sense. There was an aloofness about him and the strict control with which he compartmentalised his life was daunting to behold. Business was his top priority; he thought nothing of flying off to New York or Sydney for a few days and had done so three times in the short period they had been married. She had tried to tell herself she didn't mind. She was glad to have Nicholas to herself for a while, but her own innate honesty forced her to admit she did miss her husband.

Last Wednesday it had been brought shockingly home to her just how much. He had left on the Monday for New York and she hadn't been expecting him back until Thursday at the soonest.

After dinner, with Nicholas fast asleep in bed, Helen, feeling oddly restless, had wandered out onto the veranda to lean against the ornate balustrade in the darkness with only the moon and stars for company.

'Well met by moonlight, fair Helena.' The deep, husky drawl made her heart lurch in her breast and, turning her head, she saw Leon.

'You aren't supposed to be back yet,' she exclaimed. Their eyes met and she shivered as one long finger brushed against her cheek, then his hand curled around the nape of her neck.

'And taking liberties with Shakespeare is frowned upon,' she tried to joke.

His hand raked up through her hair and he smiled, his dark head bent towards her. 'You're right, I would much rather take liberties with you.' Sliding his other arm around her waist, he kissed her. When they finally came up for air his dark eyes held hers, and she was powerless to look away, powerless to hide her own need.

'Ah, Helen, my sweet Helen, I missed you.' His sensuous lips curled in a soft, tender smile, the sort she had only ever seen him bestow on Nicholas. Emotion threatened to choke her and she could not speak. 'And I do believe you missed me,' he prompted huskily, and her answer was in the luminous depths of her violet eyes.

They made love that night with tenderness and a passion that Helen had never experienced before. Later, cradled in his arms with her head on his chest, the steady, rhythmic beat of his heart music to her ears, she finally accepted what she had known deep down all along.

She loved Leon. The desire, the passion might be just sex to him, but it was never just sex to her. She loved him with every breath she took and she knew she always would.

He was not the hard, uncaring man she had imagined him to be. Anna and all the staff adored him, and as for Nicholas, he worshipped him. The cold, austere persona Leon presented to the world vanished as soon as he set eyes on Nicholas. He was wonderful with the boy, and lately she had the growing feeling his relaxed, caring side was extending to her. God, she hoped so! She vowed to do everything in her power to make a success of their marriage in the hope that eventually Leon might grow to love her as she loved him.

Thinking about that night now, standing in a shop waiting for Mary, Helen sighed. Her husband was a hard, complex man and a complete workaholic, but to give him his due he did always kiss her awake, and sometimes more, before descending to the basement gym for a workout. He was terrifically physically fit, but he had to be for his punishing schedule. By the time Helen got down for breakfast with Nicholas he was usually leaving or had already left, returning in the evening to spend at least an hour with Nicholas before he went to bed.

Dining alone with Leon was no longer the ordeal she had once feared. But underneath the casual conversation there was always a simmering sexual tension that Helen could not deny, didn't want to. The thought of the night ahead was ever present in her mind, for in Leon's arms she became vibrantly alive and under his tutelage increasingly sexually adventurous in a way that she had never thought herself capable of.

Helen had tried to convince herself it was simply a natural response to a long overdue sexual awakening on her part, and had nothing to do with love, but after last Wednesday night she couldn't pretend any more.

She loved him, she could not help herself. He was a wonderful, inventive lover, generous to a fault, concentrating on her pleasure in myriad ways she had never imagined possible, before seeking his own.

When he wanted to be, she had discovered much to her surprise, he was an intelligent, witty conversationalist. He had an uncanny knack for giving a thumbnail sketch of people with a subtle humour that appealed to her. She had also discovered they had the same taste in music and shared the same love of books, Leon preferring political thrillers while Helen preferred a good detective novel.

When he had realised while reading Nicholas a bedtime story that they were her humorous illustrations all the way through the book he had laughed aloud.

'My God, Helen, your talents are truly limitless,' he had quipped and kissed her, much to Nicholas' disgust.

Their conversations were naturally quite often about Nicholas, and of course discussing any arrangements Leon had made for their social life. So far they had shared Sunday lunch with Mary and her family and sometimes they went out as a foursome for dinner, all of which Helen had enjoyed, and a couple of formal dinners with some of his business acquaintances and their wives, which she had not enjoyed quite as much.

The party he was hosting tomorrow night was to introduce Helen to the distant relatives and social élite of Athens who had not been invited to the wedding. It was to be held in a top Athenian hotel and Leon had given her strict instructions this morning to buy something new to wear, which she had rather resented.

She had given up on the practical cotton nightshirts weeks ago, and indulged her secret pleasure in delicate underwear, and she had a perfectly good wardrobe of classic clothes. Helen was not quite the prim little stay-at-home Leon seemed to think she had been. She had led an active if limited social life, Nicholas permitting, as a member of a local drama group and book club. When her parents were alive they had led a busy social life in Switzerland, and Helen had learnt how to behave in any society. Her mother had taught her the fundamentals of style for a small woman when she was a young teenager and in fact she still had quite a few of her mother's classic designer clothes, which she had kept originally as mementoes and now wore. In fairness to Leon, he always complimented her on what she did wear. Plus the first time he had been away on business when he had returned he had taken her to the bank, opened an account for her, and presented her with a limitless credit card.

She had tried to refuse but, for once his cynicism not in

evidence he had rather dryly confessed he hated shopping and was hopeless at buying presents, but he wanted her and Nicholas to have everything they desired. Then he had presented her with a fabulous emerald and diamond ring he'd told her he had bought as he'd happened to be passing Van Cleef and Arpel in New York. That Leon, her workaholic husband, who by his own admission hated shopping, had found time in his busy schedule to nip into Van Cleef's just for her was what delighted her, and gave her hope that their relationship was growing into something more than just a convenience.

'So what do you think? Will I knock Chris' socks off at the party tomorrow night?' Mary did a twirl as she walked out of the dressing room.

'It won't be his socks coming off, but that apology for a dress.' Helen laughed, eyeing the clinging full-length, backless indigo-blue dress that Mary was almost falling out of.

'Too much, hmm?'

'Too little,' Helen shot back.

'You're right, but it would be great on you. Come on try it on. You have to impress the guests tomorrow night.'

Helen kissed Nicholas goodnight, and left, his comment that she looked like a lovely purple lollipop, good enough to eat, echoing in her head. She stood in front of the mirror in the master suite and eyed her reflection. Why did she let first a child and then Mary tell her what she should wear? Because she was a sucker when it came to pleasing the people she cared about, she concluded. Though no one could call this gown childish she thought ruefully; she had never worn anything so revealing in her life.

The spaghetti-strapped dress cupped her breasts, exposed her back to the waist and clung to her hips and thighs like a second skin. The fantail pleat in the back was there out of necessity, allowing her to walk. But at least this time she was wearing a pair of four-inch high-heeled diamanté sandals, favourites of hers. And with Anna's help her hair was piled in an elegant concoction of curls on the top of her head, making her look quite tall, she told herself bracingly.

'*Theos,* you are not going out in that.' Leon's voice cut into her musings, and she turned her head to see him exit the dressing room and walk towards her.

The breath stopped in her throat. He looked strikingly attractive in a formal black dinner suit, and the predatory expression in the dark eyes that roamed blatantly over her set her pulse racing.

'Don't you approve?' She pouted and did a swift twirl. 'Mary said it was definitely me.' She grinned cheekily up at him.

Leon gasped, a certain part of his body leaping to immediate attention. The view of her back naked to her pert bum was enough to make a strong man weak at the knees.

'Mary wants her head examined,' he said when he could finally speak, taking in her beautiful smiling face and the shining mass of fair curls pinned on the top of her head. She was wearing a shimmering sort of purple-blue dress that curved across her perfect breasts, revealing more of the creamy smooth fullness than any man except him should ever see, he thought proprietorially. And what was left of the gown clung to every curve of her delectable body.

A wry smile quirked his mouth. 'That dress is verging on the indecent, but you look absolutely stunning.' Moving towards her, he dropped a kiss on the tip of her nose.

'Thank you, kind sir,' she quipped. 'But Nicholas thinks I look like a purple lollipop and good enough to eat.'

'That boy has great taste for a child.' Leon chuckled and reached for her shoulders. 'And I definitely agree with him,' he husked and drew her gently against his tall frame. 'I wouldn't mind eating you right here and now.' The thought of lowering his head to the delta of her thighs and tasting her sweetness rendered him rock-hard.

She lifted sparkling eyes to his, and he saw her pupils darken and dilate. He slipped a hand around her neck and watched as her eyelids drifted down, her lips softly parting in anticipation of his kiss.

'I don't dare or we will never get out of here,' he groaned, and abruptly he dropped one hand to her tiny waist and spun her back to face the mirror.

'What do you think?'

Helen felt the coldness on her skin and upon seeing her re-flection in the glass her eyes widened in amazement at the fabulous fall of diamonds strung around her throat. She lifted her hand and touched the jewels, lifting her eyes to meet his in the mirror.

'Leon,' she murmured his name, overwhelmed by his gift. 'You bought this for me?'

He smiled slightly. 'Yes, our six week anniversary. Do you like it?'

'I love it,' she said truthfully, stunned that he had cared enough to actually remember how many weeks they had been married. 'It is the most fabulous gift I have ever received. Thank you.'

She had to blink away an emotional tear. Then she remem-bered. 'But I thought you never went shopping for presents.'

'I had some help,' he confessed ruefully, and, wrapping his arms around her stomach, he pulled her back against the hard warmth of his body. 'I asked Mary to make sure you bought a dress and to tell me what kind of jewellery would match. She said to stick to diamonds, making it easy for me.' Loosening his hold on her, he slipped his hand in his jacket pocket. 'I bought the earrings and bracelet to match.' He clipped the bracelet around her slender wrist. 'You can manage the earrings yourself, I hope.' He placed them in her hand. 'Because if I hold you much longer that is it, we will be going nowhere.'

Helen had felt the pressure of his arousal against her and a gleam of mischief sparkled in her eyes.

'That's fine by me.'

She turned and looped her arms around his neck. 'I would much prefer to stay here.' She pressed up against him and tilted back her head to look up into his darkening eyes. 'Parties are not my scene. I much prefer one to one,' she declared softly, her full lips curving in a slow, sensual smile.

'No, you don't, you little witch, I am not being side-tracked,' he declared with a reluctant smile. 'But hold that thought until we return, hmm?'

His unexpected gift and commanding presence at her side gave her the confidence to stand at the entrance to the grand ballroom and greet all the guests.

With Leon's arm around her Helen glanced up at him, her violet eyes sparkling. 'I feel like royalty standing here. Do we have to do this?'

'Not for much longer,' he murmured, and then someone called his name and his arm suddenly tightened around her waist.

'Takis, nice to see you. I wasn't sure you would make it.'

Helen cast a sidelong glance at Leon, immediately sensing he was not pleased to see the man at all. Then she looked at the man standing in front of them, her eyes widening in instinctive female appreciation. He was of medium height, slim with black hair and strikingly handsome in a rakish kind of way.

'I wouldn't miss your wedding party for the world. I attended your first one, remember?' the man drawled.

He looked Greek, but he spoke with an American accent, Helen noted, and then he smiled and his brown eyes gleamed golden as they met hers.

'So this is Helen.' Taking her unresisting hand, he lifted it to his lips. 'It is a pleasure to meet you, and a surprise. I never thought Leon had such good taste, stick-like models are more his scene. But you, babe, you are exquisite, a perfect little Barbie doll.'

Helen was still trying to decide if it was an insult or a compliment to be called a babe and a Barbie doll in the same sentence when he turned his attention back to Leon.

'A beautiful wife and a son as well—you are a lucky bastard, cousin.'

'Thank you, Takis,' Leon said smoothly. 'I knew you would be pleased for me. Now if you will excuse us, it is time we mingled.'

She wasn't imagining it; the tension between the two men was palpable. Helen glanced curiously at her husband but before she could utter a word he was urging her into the crowd.

'Wait a minute.' She stopped. 'What was all that about? Why didn't you tell that man Nicholas isn't your son, but Delia's?'

'Why bother?' He shrugged one shoulder. 'He is our son now, or had you forgotten at the sight of a handsome face?' he prompted silkily.

'No...' Helen shook her head. 'And don't pretend you're jealous,' she mocked, while secretly hugging the thought to her. 'But I am surprised. I mean, he is your cousin—surely he knows.'

'Actually, strictly speaking he is my late wife's cousin, and I am sure he does know. He is the sort who makes it his business to know everything. But Nicholas is no concern of his.'

'If you say so,' Helen murmured, but she could not help recalling quite a few odd glances from different people over the past few weeks that she had put down to natural curiosity, now she wasn't so sure.

'I've noticed some peculiar looks from a few people, even Mary on our wedding day.' She raised puzzled eyes to his. 'I suppose it is the family likeness between Nicholas and yourself. But shouldn't you deny the assumption? I mean, we don't want to mislead people.'

'Helen, darling,' he drawled with a sardonic lift of one ebony brow, 'it is public knowledge that both you and I have stated Nicholas is my sister's child. But people believe what they want to believe.' His firm lips twisted in a wry smile. 'As far as I am concerned I couldn't care less what other people think. The boy knows the truth, that is all that matters.'

'Yes, but—'

'So they assume you're his mother—what difference does it make?' And his arm tightened around her. 'In life as in business it is sometimes beneficial to muddy the waters a little. And if it is your reputation you are worried about, forget it. As my wife you are beyond reproach, and if the confusion helps Delia's reputation in other people's eyes—why not? Nicholas might thank us for it in years to come.'

Helen frowned. He sounded so reasonable, but he was protecting the memory of his sister at the expense of hers. Well, not exactly, she conceded. He hadn't actually lied. Leon just manipulated the situation, allowing people to think what they wanted to think. Much the same as he had with her when he had suggested a marriage of convenience. He had to have known what she'd thought, and she wondered how many more false assumptions he had allowed her to make.

Not much later she found out.

Helen glanced around the glittering throng not feeling quite so confident. Waiters circled the crowd with drinks and canapés, a quintet played dance music and everyone looked to be enjoying themselves.

'Love the necklace.' The familiar voice of Mary drew Helen's attention to the couple who had stopped in front of them. She saw her friend flick a glance at Leon.

'It is perfect, Leon,' Mary declared and grinned at Helen. 'I gave him such detailed instructions even he could not fail. You really have me to thank for his choice,' she declared outrageously. Everyone laughed, Helen included, relieved at Mary's timely interruption.

Leon was right. She was worrying about nothing, what did it matter what a few people thought? Helen shot him a teasing glance. 'Surely you are not going to let Mary get away with insulting you.'

'Her husband is my lawyer. Trust me, if I say a word to Mary he will sue me,' Leon replied drolly, and more laughter ensued.

Chris stopped a passing waiter and champagne was served all around. He then insisted, as this was an official wedding party, albeit the second one, he had to make a toast.

'To two good friends, Helen and Leon, may you have a long and happy marriage.'

'Thank you,' Leon replied sincerely and, looking into the vividly sparkling eyes of his wife, he suddenly realised he didn't care that she had kept his nephew hidden for years, didn't care if she had known about the money she was to inherit. She was worth every penny and more. He thanked God and Delia that he had found her, and had had the good sense to marry her.

She gave him a brilliant smile, and his chest tightened as his hand automatically flexed on her waist with the sudden stirring in his groin. How she did this to him he couldn't explain and he didn't care, he simply relished the feeling.

A strong sense of elation gripped him. The nearest he had

ever come to feeling like this was when he clinched a particularly good deal. But even the best deal of his life did not compare with the heady pleasure he felt right now with Helen openly gazing up at him with adoration in her gorgeous eyes for all to see.

He was not a demonstrative man, never had been. His mother had knocked that tendency out of him as a child with her violent mood swings, one day loving him and the next day cursing him, so he had learnt very early in life not to trust emotions of any kind. But now with all his friends and acquaintances around him he declared, 'And the biggest thank you must go to my beautiful wife for being brave enough to take on a cynic like me for her husband.' And dipping his head, he kissed her. He felt her sway against him, tasted the melting sweetness of her mouth, and very reluctantly broke the kiss, while quickly calculating how much longer they would have to stay for propriety's sake.

CHAPTER TEN

A MINUTE LATER Leon cursed silently under his breath. Dropping his hand from Helen's waist, he squared his broad shoulders, and went still. There was tension in every line of his body, his grin fading to a grimace as his dark eyes rested on two late arrivals. The French Ambassador to Greece, who had been invited with his wife, but instead had turned up with a different companion, a very tall, striking-looking woman... Louisa...

What the hell was she doing here? He had broken up with her the week before he'd married. And she had done very well out of the deal. He had given her a luxury apartment in Paris and a considerable amount of money in consolation for his ending their affair.

'M. Distel, a pleasure to see you again.' Leon shook the man's hand. 'Louisa.' He nodded at his ex-lover but he could do nothing to prevent the usual French greeting of a kiss on both cheeks by the woman, one of which darted to his mouth. Then reluctantly but smoothly he introduced the pair to Helen.

Helen had immediately stiffened sensing danger the minute Leon's hand had fallen from her waist. She had felt his tension, and, following the direction of his eyes had watched the very tall, glamorous-looking woman walking towards them. Her hair a mixture of brown and red stripes, was perfectly cut in a short asymmetrical chop, and the black dress she wore was obviously the latest in designer chic and very short too, exposing her incredibly long legs.

But it was her face Helen noticed most. Her dark eyes, kohl-rimmed and narrow, were fixed on Leon like heat seeking missiles, her lush lips, obviously collagen-enhanced, Helen thought distastefully, curved in an intimate smile just for him. And when Leon said her name the red-nailed hand she laid on his arm screamed possession. The kisses she planted on him confirmed how close they were.

Feminine intuition, every instinct, told Helen that this woman had known Leon in the most intimate way possible, and the happy little bubble she had been floating in for the last few weeks burst, pierced by the dual monsters of suspicion and jealousy. It was easy to forget locked in her husband's arms that he had quite a few lovers in his past, but to be faced with one of them made it impossible to ignore. She accepted the congratulations of the French ambassador in a cool calm voice, but when Louisa took her hand and smiled with dark, spite-filled eyes her composure almost deserted her.

'So you're the lucky lady, not at all what I expected.' The woman stared down at Helen, making her feel like a midget, and it only got worse as she added. 'You are really quite small.'

'Ah, small but perfect.' The Frenchman intervened with true Gallic charm. 'And you also have a son, I believe, a great gift for any man.'

Helen heard Mary gasp at her side, but by a terrific effort of will she retained her self-control, while inside she was fuming.

'Not my son—' she glanced up at Leon her eyes diamond bright '—is he, darling?'

Leon let his eyes rest for a moment on Helen. She was angry and hurt and he didn't blame her. He had dismissed her worry over the parenthood of the boy quite casually after Takis' comment, and now Distel was implying the same. She was so lovely and so naive in a worldly sense he should have realised she was sensitive about the boy's parenthood, whereas he didn't give a damn one way or the other. But if he wasn't very careful the sophisticated French pair would make mincemeat of her in a second if he let them. Louisa had already insulted his wife with her crack about her height; he knew Helen was touchy on the subject. Why, he had no idea, she was perfect in his eyes.

But for once in his life he felt fiercely protective and embarrassed at the same time, not emotions he was familiar with. He knew most of the people here recognised Louisa as his ex-mistress, and he felt guilty that his past affair had put Helen in this position and was determined to remedy the situation, before she had a chance to find out.

With that in mind he said, 'No, of course not, Helen. Everyone knows he is my sister Delia's child. But the ambassador's English is not so good.' He smiled gently down at her. 'Excuse me for a moment while I explain to him in French, hmm…' She nodded her head and he returned his attention to Distel and Louisa.

The patronising swine, Helen thought, and shook her head, too enraged to speak. Instead she took another glass of champagne from a passing waiter, and listened. Her face paled and the blood turned to ice in her veins, her suspicions confirmed. She needed to sit down or she would fall down, such was the extent of her shock. Swiftly she drained the glass and when Mary moved to visit the powder room Helen jumped at the chance to go with her. She had heard enough, more than enough.

'That woman is Leon's lover,' Helen said flatly as they entered the powder room.

'No, you're wrong,' Mary quickly denied—a little too quickly.

Helen looked at her friend with cold, dull eyes. 'Please don't bother to lie on my account, it is not necessary.'

'I'm not exactly lying.' Mary sighed. 'But I'm not surprised you guessed they had had an affair. Louisa made it pretty obvious she couldn't take her eyes off him. But really, Helen, you have nothing to worry about. Leon married you. He loves you and I know the affair is over. Chris told me so.'

'And you believed him.' Helen shook her head and sank down on the nearest chair, not sure her legs would support her. She was numb with shock. She knew Leon did not love her, but to be so callous as to allow his mistress to kiss him in front of her was beyond belief. But then what did she know about men, or the society Leon moved in, other than it was far too sophisticated and blasé for her? she thought bitterly, and glanced up at her hovering friend.

'I hate to tell you, Mary, but your husband lied, and before you say anything else I should tell you I speak excellent French and I understood every word they said.'

Mary collapsed in the chair beside her. 'You speak French. Oh, no. But wait a second, he only spoke for a moment, then the ambassador and Louisa chipped in,' Mary exclaimed. 'They'd only been speaking for a few minutes before we left. So what on earth was said that upset you so quickly?'

Helen folded her arms across her chest, her hands rubbing her upper arms. She was shivering and the cold went bone deep.

'Enough, more than enough. Leon explained Nicholas was his sister's child and then asked Distel if his wife was indisposed.' Helen relayed the gist of the conversation in a harsh, colourless voice. 'The Frenchman said yes, and rather sarcastically added he didn't think Leon would mind him bringing Louisa because he knew they were such old close friends.' She glanced back at Mary. 'The French language lends itself beautifully to sarcasm—did you know that?'

'I'm not interested in the language. Tell me what happened next.'

'Louisa intervened, and said to Leon, and I quote, "Really, *mon cher,* you have nothing to worry about. I would not dream of upsetting your little wife by telling her about us. I know you only married her for the child. I remember in every intimate detail the last night we spent together the week before your wedding. And ten days ago when you gave me the deeds to the apartment, such an extravagant gift..."'

Helen paused for a moment and blinked to hold back the tears that threatened, then carried on stoically. '"I knew it was to ease your conscience, after almost four years I understand you perfectly, *cher,* and when you come back as usual I can promise you will enjoy seeing and removing what your generosity bought." At which point she laughed and you gave me an excuse to leave to come to the powder room, for which I am eternally grateful,' Helen concluded.

'What a bitch.'

'My sentiments exactly,' Helen agreed. 'But a perfect match for my lying bastard of a husband. He is obviously still seeing her. He told me he was going to New York, but according to that woman he saw her in Paris ten days ago.'

'You don't know that.' Mary tried to comfort her. 'You never heard Leon's reply. He probably denied Louisa's whole scenario. Why, only moments earlier Leon, who has never been given to overt displays of affection in his life, thanked you for marrying him and kissed you in front of everyone. That must mean something; you have to give him a chance.'

Helen rose to her feet, her face white and her usually expressive eyes curiously blank. 'I don't think so,' she responded bluntly.

'Oh, come on, Helen, you can't believe for a minute Leon would prefer a hard-faced, stick-thin glamour puss like her to you. You are beautiful and caring and kind. Whereas that one is so up herself I wouldn't mind betting her Brazilian wax is striped red to match her hair.'

'That is terrible.' But the picture Mary painted did make Helen's lips quirk at the corners.

'But you almost smiled.' Mary stood up and rested her hand on Helen's arm. 'Come on, let's get back in there. You are not going to let a bitch like Louisa upset you. And if there is anything I can do…'

'Don't worry, Mary.' Helen glanced at her friend, and, seeing the compassion in her gaze, almost gave in to the pain of the grief that she knew was waiting for her.

But she had too much experience of life's hard knocks to succumb. The loss of her parents, the loss of her eyesight for over a year, the loss of her ability to bear children, the loss of her grandfather and the loss of her best friend had taught her all the tears in the world did not help. 'I will be fine and I won't cause a scene. You're right, it is time we rejoined the party.'

'You're sure?'

'Positive,' Helen said, and opened the door. She felt curiously detached as she walked back into the ballroom. The sound of the crowd, the laughter, the music, could not penetrate the coldness that had settled around her like an invisible cloak. Nothing had really changed she told herself. She still had Nicholas. She had always known Leon was a womanising devil; his own sister had intimated as much. As for loving the man—not any more.

Leon was right: love was an illusion, an illusion she had suffered from for a brief period of time, and could now forget. She had cried at the loss of her family and her friend. All worthy people who had cared for her, but her husband wasn't worth a single tear.

* * *

There was no sign of the French couple when they re-entered the ballroom. Chris and Leon were standing to one side of the dance floor, deep in conversation, but both male heads turned in unison as Mary with Helen behind her entered the ballroom.

Leon's dark gaze sought Helen's and in the very next second he realised something was wrong. Her lips parted over her small white teeth, but the smile she gave him was brittle and never reached her eyes.

He stepped towards her and looped an arm around her waist. 'I missed you,' he whispered softly and brushed her lips with his own. She did not respond, she simply stood still in his hold. 'I have a strong desire to dance with you.' He tried again, lowering his head to breathe against her small ear. 'I simply want you in my arms.'

'Sorry. Mary and I were talking.'

He put both arms around her and drew her onto the dance floor, and she made no objection. She placed her small hand on his shoulder and let him guide her to the music, but something was different.

'Are you all right?' He nuzzled her ear, and she turned her head away.

'Of course. Why wouldn't I be?'

She kept her beautiful face averted, she wouldn't look at him. He tightened his hold on her but her gorgeous body wasn't softening against his as he had come to expect. She was physically in his arms, but mentally miles away.

'Did Mary say something to upset you?' he demanded.

'No.'

He stroked a hand up her naked back, his fingers trailing the indentation of her spine, but she stayed rigid in his arms, and for a moment an unknown emotion went through him— primarily anger, but incredibly laced with fear. No, he was imagining things. Helen was putty in his hands, but she was also quite shy in public. This glittering affair was probably a bit of an ordeal for her, he rationalised her odd behaviour. Of course she was tense as the object of all eyes.

He folded her closer into him. 'Relax, you are the most beautiful woman here and everyone adores you.'

You certainly don't, Helen wanted to scream. But instead she said curtly, 'I doubt that.'

She flicked a cold glance at his hard face and just as quickly away again. Did he really think she was such a wimp she needed reassurance from an arrogant, lying toad like him? Though in one respect Leon had been right all along; the fever in her blood when he touched her was as he had said, just sex. Thankfully she no longer felt anything in his arms. His betrayal had killed every finer emotion in her stone-dead.

His hand curved around her nape, and tilted her head back so she was forced to look at him.

'Are you sure you are okay? We don't have to stay much longer if you don't want to.'

'I wouldn't dream of leaving early. I intend to dance the night away.' She sent him a glittering smile and linked her hands behind his neck. When what she really wanted to do was choke the faithless swine. Anger was the only emotion she had left.

Helen slid into the limo and as far away from Leon as she could get and, leaning back, closed her eyes. She didn't want to look at him, and she certainly didn't want to speak to him. She had danced and laughed all night, and he had had the nerve to tell her she had been the belle of the ball. What a snake. He had the emotional sensitivity of a boa constrictor, but she was determined he was not going to squeeze the life out of her.

She was her own woman, deserving of honour and respect,

and without that they had nothing. She had been fooling herself for weeks, but no more.

When the limo stopped she leapt straight out and into the house and upstairs without stopping. Once in the master suite she took the diamonds from her throat and dropped them where she stood along with the earrings and bracelet, and, turning, headed for the dressing room. She heard him enter the bedroom as she removed the pins from her hair, and shaking her head, she let it fall down to her shoulders. She opened a drawer and avoiding the more glamorous night-wear, she selected a nightshirt. Discarding the dress, she pulled it over her head and walked back into the bedroom.

Leon was standing in the middle of the room, without his jacket and tie, his shirt unbuttoned to his waist and in his hand the jewels she had dropped on the floor. She glanced at his face but when he came towards her she backed away instinctively.

He stopped, his chiselled features hardening with something like anger. 'Rather careless, dropping these on the floor. Are you going to tell me what this is all about, Helen? I don't appreciate a woman who blows hot and cold. I was beginning to think better of you, but obviously I was mistaken, unless you have some explanation for acting out of character all evening.'

'And what would you know about my character? You think you know me so well simply because we share a bed and body fluids, but you don't know me at all,' she shot back with scathing bluntness. 'If you did, you might have realised I spent the first fourteen years of my life in Switzerland. They speak four different languages there, and I am fluent in two of them: Italian and French. Need I say more?' She saw a dark flush spread across his high cheekbones. He had a good right to look guilty, the no-good, cheating waster.

'Ah.' He shoved the jewels in his trouser pocket. 'You

heard Louisa.' His dark, compelling eyes held hers as he lessened the space between them. 'That was careless of me and bad mannered, but I switched to French thinking to spare you any embarrassment.'

'You're all heart,' she jeered.

His reply was to reach for her and pull her against him. 'You heard she was once my mistress and for that I am sorry.' His lips curved in a hateful smile. 'But you have no need to be jealous, Helen. I put an end to it before we married, and as long as I have you I don't want any other woman, I swear.'

His truly astounding, unbelievable conceit was too much for Helen and she exploded with rage. 'You must think I am crazy if you expect me to believe a word you say. You are the most devious, manipulative, arrogant swine it has ever been my misfortune to meet. My God, you have been having an affair with that woman for years. What kind of fool do you take me for? The week before you married me you were in her bed. You actually told me you had a pressing engagement in Paris. You didn't mention pressing the flesh, but I should have known. Delia told me what a faithless lot the men in her family were, and, by heaven, she was right. You even had the cheek to tell me you were going to New York and then visited that woman straight from my bed ten days ago, a bed where you had the gall to call me *ma petite,* a French term, when we first had sex.' She would not call it love.

'Now I know why—force of habit,' she jeered. 'Then to cap it all I discover you have given your lover an apartment and Lord knows what else. And you wonder why the jewels you gave me ended up on the floor.' She shook her head in utter rejection of him.

'Are you quite finished assassinating my character?' Leon

demanded harshly, placing a steel-like arm around her waist
and hauling her hard against him.

She looked up at him with blazing violet eyes. 'God help
Nicholas with you as his father; you haven't a moral bone in
your body. As for me, I never want you to touch me again.'

Her last crack was too much for Leon. He was no saint, and
he was guilty of having sex with Louisa the week before his
wedding. Mainly because when he had made it very clear their
affair was finally over she had stripped naked and begged him
to make love to her one last time. He had certainly not slept
with her, and had left before midnight. Ungallant maybe, but
true. Her appearance tonight at the party had been none of his
doing, but that his wife should think so badly of him, to
believe that he had lied when he'd said he was going to New
York, was an insult too far.

He hauled her closer and plunged his hand into her hair and
jerked her head back to capture her angry mouth with his. He
thrust into the hot, moist depths with an urgent, angry passion.
He felt her resistance and fought down the primitive urge to
bury himself deep inside her, and make her realise she was
his in the most basic way.

Instead with a terrific effort he gentled the fury of his kiss.
But still she remained rigid in his arms. Fired by anger and
frustration, he slipped a hand beneath her shirt, tracing the line
of her leg and thigh while he lowered his head and caught her
breast through the fine fabric of her shirt.

Suddenly the cloak of detachment, the numbness that had
helped Helen through the evening, shattered, leaving in its
place a raw, aching pain. Her heart thundered in her breast and
she lashed wildly out at him, but it was like hitting a brick
wall. Though she fought like a wild woman, when his mouth
and teeth fed on her breast the dampness of the fabric rubbing
against her sensitive nipples made every sensual receptor in

her body quiver and burn. The savage sensuality of his kiss as he captured her mouth again and the caressing stroke of his hand roaming over her hip and the apex of her thighs with a familiarity her body recognised ignited a burning need inside her, even as her mind rejected him.

He picked her up and dropped her naked on the bed, when she had lost the nightshirt she had no idea. All she was aware of was the heat, the weight, the scent of him above her. A muscled leg parted hers, his hungry mouth clamping on her pouting breast, and finally her body arched convulsively and she was conscious of nothing except the thick length of him thrusting, filling her with ever-deeper strokes, until she was swept away in a maelstrom of shuddering ecstatic sensations that culminated in an explosion of the senses so heart stoppingly intense that for a moment she ceased to breathe.

She felt Leon's weight roll off her, and wondered if that was the little death she had read about as they lay beside each other in silence, the only sounds the heavy pounding of hearts and ragged breathing.

Helen had nothing to say. Her body had made a liar of her.

Leon rose up on one elbow and looked down into her shadowed eyes. 'I think we can safely forget your, "I never want you to touch me again,"' he taunted softly. 'You can no more resist the passion, the desire, that flares between us than I can.'

'That is your conceited opinion,' she shot back.

'Not an opinion, fact, and to prove my point I won't touch you again, until *you* ask me,' he stated, his lips curling in a derisive smile. 'And I doubt I will have to wait long. Some women, once they get a taste for sex, can't do without, and I have a feeling you fall into that category, Helen.'

'In your dreams,' she spat. Shamed at her own weakness and hating him all over again, she wanted to hit out at him, dent his massive ego. 'I am here for Nicholas and nothing else, and, just to set the record straight, the scar on my belly is not from an appendectomy, but from an accident. So if you are nursing any illusion I might get pregnant one day, forget it. I can't have children.'

In her distress and anger she revealed her deepest secret, but his reaction was not what she expected.

His dark gaze narrowed to rest on her face for a long moment and then his hand stroked gently down her body, one long finger tracing the scar, and when he lifted his head again the dark eyes that met hers held a strange light, and his mouth had an ironic twist to it for all that it was set in a straight line.

'A biological child of my own really does not matter to me. We have Nicholas,' he said coolly. 'What happened tonight was unfortunate, and I don't expect you to believe me unreservedly. But if you had listened a little longer you would have heard me reminding Louisa that our affair was definitely over, as she knew perfectly well, and she had been paid off quite handsomely for her friendship. You have nothing to worry about; forget it ever happened.'

His easy dismissal of her confession infuriated Helen still further. Her inability to have a child was and would be a lifelong regret to Helen, but Leon was so cool, so unfazed by her announcement, he obviously didn't give a jot for her feelings. She could almost feel sorry for the French woman, but not quite.

'Is that what your first wife did when she found out about your lovers? Or did Tina never find out what a two-timing bastard you are? Did you simply lie to her as you lied to me when you said you were faithful to her?' she asked bitterly.

'I never lied to you, or Tina, not that she would have cared if I did,' he stated with a slightly cynical smile. 'Tina was a law unto herself. I was twenty-three when I met her and I married her because she would not let me into her bed until I did.'

And for her father's bank, according to Delia, Helen thought distastefully.

'Before you ask,' Leon continued, accurately reading her mind, 'the merger with her father's bank was of much greater benefit to him than it was to us. We were looking to expand into America, true, but there were much more viable options on the table than his, and I had to work like a slave to make the merger profitable.

'As for the rest, I told you the truth when I said I was faithful to Tina as long as she was to me.' His wry mocking glance seared through her as he continued. 'What I didn't tell you, as I do not like to malign the departed, was that although Tina was a lovely lady I was not her first lover and I certainly was not her last. The concept of monogamy was totally foreign to her nature.'

Helen's lips tightened. *And his,* she thought savagely.

'I am not in the habit of explaining my past actions to anyone, but in this case I will make an exception, because I can tell by the expression on your face that like all females you are never going to let the matter drop until I do,' he said cynically. 'By the time you met Tina in Greece we had been married seven years and she had had at least three lovers that I knew of, Takis, her cousin the party animal, being one of them. Adultery is not the sole prerogative of the man in any marriage. We stayed married mainly for the sake of our fathers as they were great friends, and also as I had no intention of ever marrying again I saw no compelling need to divorce. If that offends your prim little mind, tough, but it is the truth.'

Helen's eyes widened incredulously on his face. Tina unfaithful to him? Why would any woman want another man once they had him? was the first thought that popped into her mind. Her second that for a man with a massive ego like Leon to freely admit his wife had cuckolded him and with her own cousin was unbelievable.

She stared up at him contemplatively. His black hair was rumpled and falling over his forehead, his great body gleamed golden in the dim light and his dark gaze was curiously intent on her face. For a moment she had the fanciful idea he actually needed her to believe him.

No. Leon didn't need anyone. As for believing him, she didn't know what to believe any more. Leon had turned her life upside down, and here she was lying beneath him sated from sex. When, if she had a grain of common sense, she would be packing her bags and leaving. So what did that make her?

A fool, she thought, but it did not stop her murmuring, 'If that is true, I am sorry.'

'No need to be, and I don't need your sympathy. It changes nothing. You and I are married with a child to care for and that is all that matters.'

He was right in one respect. Unless she left Nicholas, and she would never do that willingly, everything else was irrelevant. She had not married Leon for his character, or for the sex. Because that was all it was or ever could be, she recognised now. Her dream of Leon growing to care for her was just that—a dream.

'I need to get up and shower, if you don't mind.'

'Ask me nicely and I'll join you.'

'Hell will freeze over first,' she snarled and rolled off the bed and raced to the bathroom with his mocking laughter ringing in her ears.

When she returned to the bedroom Leon was sprawled across the wide bed, flat on his back and sound asleep. She looked at him for a long time. He really was quite magnificent—on a sexual level, perfect. But was she mature or jaded enough to accept sex for fun, and nothing more? She was still worrying the thought in her mind when she crawled into bed.

When she awoke the next morning he was gone, and she

realised for the first time he had slept beside her without touching her, and left without the early-morning kiss he usually gave her. Obviously he had meant what he had said about not touching her until she asked him. Well she never would, she silently vowed.

When he returned that night it was as if nothing had changed. Over dinner he told her they were leaving for the island the following day for two weeks over the Easter holiday, and the nanny was having a few days leave but would join them later.

When he joined her in bed he simply said goodnight, turned his back on her and within minutes the deep even sound of his breathing told her he was asleep. Sleep did not come so easy for Helen. The seed of hope that had taken root in her heart and begun to grow in the last few weeks had, like a tender shoot caught by a spring frost, been killed stone-dead.

The next day they boarded a much smaller aircraft than the company jet necessary to land on the island's private runway. Nicholas was ecstatic, Helen subdued and Leon his usual aloof self.

CHAPTER ELEVEN

'I HAVE TO go to the mainland this morning.' Leon addressed his wife over the breakfast table set on the terrace of the villa. She looked up at him her violet eyes wary, and he wanted to shake her. No, what he actually wanted to do was make mad, passionate love to her, and he cursed for the hundredth time the asinine challenge he had made that she had to ask him first. He must have been mad, but his pride would not let him back down.

She would come around he knew. He could see the desire in her eyes, when she watched him covertly beneath those incredible long lashes, in the way she backed away from him when they were alone in the bedroom or when they messed about near naked on the beach with Nicholas. Helen was frightened to touch him, and he was man enough to know she was more afraid of herself than him.

It was only a matter of time before she gave in and begged him to make love to her. In the meantime, unless he wanted to end up looking like a prune from the countless cold showers, he needed to get off the island and away from temptation for a few hours. Thankfully, he had some business to discuss with Chris.

'I have meetings lined up with Chris. You can come with me if you like.' Where the hell had that come from? And he told himself he was relieved when she refused.

* * *

After over a week of Leon's constant company, it was with a relieved sigh that Helen stretched out on a towel on the beach.

She had spent a fun day with Nicholas, a visit to the harbour and an attempt at fishing, followed by lunch outside the local café. A slow walk back to the villa, and a short nap, and now it was three in the afternoon and she had given in to his demand to play on the beach.

She glanced at Nicholas happily building a sandcastle a few feet away and sighed. At least he was enjoying the holiday, but the sight of a Leon wearing a tee shirt and shorts day after day, or even less on the beach with them, had her nerves in shreds. It was bad enough she had to fight the temptation to touch him in the huge bed at night, without being faced with his great bronzed body all day as well.

'When is Dad coming back?' Nicholas demanded, coming to slump down on the towel beside her. 'I want him to give me another swimming lesson.'

'I can do that,' Helen declared and got to her feet. She threw off her sun hat and caught his hand in hers. 'Women are just as good as men at swimming, you know. I don't want you growing up to be a chauvinist.' Like Leon, she thought as she led him towards the water.

'What is a chauvest…chauvinct…?'

'Yes, what is a chauvinist?' a light voice called.

Helen spun around, her eyes widening. 'Mary, where did you come from?'

She was walking towards her with her eldest son Mark at her side.

'Leon brought us all over, along with the nanny. He thought you might like some female company for the Easter weekend and the children would enjoy playing together.'

'It's great to see you, and he's right, I could use the company, but he never said anything to me.'

'Maybe he wanted to surprise you.' Mary grinned and, with an order to Mark to watch Nicholas, turned her keen gaze on Helen. 'I can see why, you are not looking very well at all. What's with the dark circles under the eyes? You are on holiday, you're supposed to be relaxing, not wound up as tight as a drum.'

Helen grimaced. 'What do you expect?' She glanced at Nicholas and saw he was happily engrossed with building the sandcastle again with Mark supervising. 'And to answer your first query, a chauvinist is a man like Leon, a man who thinks women are an inferior species, and the only place for them is in bed.'

'That bad, hmm?' Mary took her arm. 'Come on, sit down I have something to tell you.'

Helen sat back down on the towel and Mary flopped down beside her.

'You love him, I can see that, and I can understand why you don't trust him after what you overheard. As a lawyer I know I should not betray a confidence, but I like to think of you as my friend and you deserve to know.'

'That sounds ominous.'

'Not at all. Chris is not just Leon's lawyer, he's also his friend. Leon called him last night to tell him he was coming over to go over some family business they had been dealing with. But he also told Chris that, although he enjoyed every moment here with you, he thought you might appreciate some female company for the weekend. Now for Leon to actually consider how a woman might feel outside of the bedroom is definitely a first in all the time Chris has known him. Chris is convinced Leon is totally smitten with you.' Mary lifted her eyebrow elegantly in Helen's direction.

'You don't need me to tell you Leon is a cynic where women are concerned. But even more crucial information I discovered later, in bed.' She grinned wickedly. 'It was Chris who visited Louisa in Paris a couple of weeks ago. It was Chris in his capacity as Leon's lawyer who presented Louisa with the deeds of the apartment, and a cheque for a large sum of money. Not very nice, I know, but not grounds for divorce. Now, whether Leon slept with Louisa the week before he married you, I don't know, but he definitely did not afterwards. He wasn't even in Paris when Chris clinched the less than salubrious deal, and that is the absolute truth. Pillow talk can be a mine of information.' Mary chuckled. 'But you must never tell a soul I told you this or Chris will kill me.'

Thinking about the conversation she had overheard, Helen realised what Mary was saying could be true. Louisa had not actually said Leon had handed the gifts over personally. Helen had just jumped to that conclusion. She looked into the eyes of her friend and saw the honesty and genuine care there and sighed.

'I believe you, Mary, but it changes nothing. Leon does not believe in love. I will never be anything other than a convenient body in his bed, and not even that now,' she confided. 'In the fight we had after the party the conceited devil declared he would not touch me again unless I asked him, and that is never going to happen.'

'Talk about cutting off your own nose to spite your own face—are you crazy?' Mary declared. 'Heaven knows, Leon has never had much love in his life and he probably would not recognise the emotion if it hit him in the face. But if you really love him, show him. What are you, a woman or a wimp? You can easily make him change his mind. It's up to you to try, and now I am taking these two boys back to the villa and you can stay here for a while to think what you really want to do.'

If Helen believed Mary, and she did, Leon had been faithful at least since they had married. But with the image of his magnificent virile body flashing though her mind, she recognised he wasn't a man cut out to be celibate, and there were hundreds of willing women out there. Was she such a fool as to deny what her body craved, and maybe push him into the arms of another woman? Not a pleasant thought, and one that made her realise sadly that she still did not trust him. Her heart told her love and trust were indivisible, but her head and her achingly frustrated body were telling her to go for the love and hope the trust came later.

Helen was still thinking what she wanted to do, or more to the point whether she dared do what her heart was telling her to, when she walked into the bedroom to shower and change. She slipped off her shirt and grimaced as the sand stuck in her bikini irritated her skin. Then her answer walked out of the bathroom, all six feet plus of vibrant male, his black hair wet from the shower and wearing only a towel slung around his lean hips.

'Leon, I thought you were with Chris and the children,' Helen blurted, her heart hammering against her breastbone, her gaze roaming helplessly over his near-naked body. In front of her fascinated gaze he whipped the towel off his hips and began rubbing his hair dry.

'The nanny is looking after them.' Leon slung the towel around his neck, his dark eyes flicking appreciatively over her bikini clad figure and up to her scarlet face. The pupils of her wide eyes were dilating with desire, and her lush little breasts were firm, the rigid nipples peaking against the scrap of blue fabric just begging to be touched.

The fact she could still blush after all they had shared was a source of amusement to him and rather endearing. He took the towel from his neck and draped it around his hips as he walked towards her and battled to control the urge to take her in his arms. With a little verbal encouragement he would not need to, she would be asking him in no time at all.

'You have the same expression on your face as the very first time you saw me naked on the beach,' he reminded her softly. 'I wanted you then, but I was married. I remember saying you should ask before ogling, that was perhaps a little unkind of me.'

He stepped forward so their bodies were only inches apart, and saw the slight tremor that shivered through her. She wanted him.

'I never saw you naked,' she returned. 'Not until we married.'

'Liar.' He smiled down into her incredible eyes. 'I saw you staring at me as you walked towards me, before I slung a towel around my waist.'

He wasn't touching her but Helen was hypnotised by his closeness the heat of his body reaching out to her. It was so long since she had felt his touch, the glory of his possession, and her whole body was flooded with heat. Mary was right, and all she had to do was ask. She opened her mouth to do just that when he continued speaking.

'Now I really appreciate you ogling me.' He let his appreciative gaze roam sensuously over her lush little body. 'And I will forgive the lie, if you say the words I want to hear. You know you want to. The tell-tale press of your perfect little nipples against your bikini top are screaming for my touch.'

Helen heard what he said and it was his damned arrogance that froze the words he wanted to hear in her throat.

'I do not lie and I did not see you naked,' she snapped. 'I was blind for over a year and I had just had my last eye operation a few weeks earlier. I was staring because I was trying to bring you into focus, and when I did you were wearing a towel,' she told him furiously.

Leon's startled gaze leapt to her face. He knew she wore disposable contact lenses and he could see she was telling the truth. *Theos,* he was fifty kinds of fool. Was he never going to get anything right with this amazing woman? Swallowing his pride, he reached for her.

'To hell with you asking, I am taking,' he declared, and hauled her against his hard body, finding her mouth with his own, and kissed her with all the pent-up frustration that had gnawed away at him for a week. He savoured the taste of her, felt her body melt against him, heard her low moan, and wondered why he had waited so long.

He swept her up in his arms, and carried her to the bed.

'What are you doing? I am covered in sand,' she squealed.

Leon grinned at her stunned expression and changed direction to head for the bathroom. 'I am going to bathe you, pamper you and make love to you, not necessarily in that order.'

Held against his broad chest Helen ran her tongue over her suddenly dry lips, and swallowed hard. He had actually said make love, and she had not had to ask him.

Unbelievably her proud, indomitable husband had relaxed his iron control and given in to his feelings. Whether it was love or lust didn't really matter. As Mary had said, it was up to Helen to teach him the difference. She looked at his hard, chiselled features, the determination and passion blazing in his eyes, and she knew even if it took a lifetime she would try, because she loved him.

When he lowered her to the cool marble floor she stood still as he deftly removed her bikini and turned on the shower. Her hungry gaze swept helplessly over him as he shed the towel and joined her.

With a gentleness that enthralled her, he bathed her from head to toe. His hands lingered in certain places and she made no objection as his lips pressed soft kisses on her sensitised flesh, igniting a familiar heat inside her. She returned the favour and ran her hands up his strong arms, caressing his wide shoulders, and clung as he lifted her from the shower to wrap her in a huge towel and tenderly dry her body.

Finally when he lowered her onto the bed, and came down on top of her, his arms either side of her supporting him, his muscular thighs trapping her legs, she felt the hard strength of his arousal against her belly and she was no longer dry, but hot, moist and wanting. His mouth covered hers and she opened to him with a passionate sigh of relief.

He lifted his head, his smouldering gaze sweeping over her. 'Have you any idea how beautiful you are?' he husked.

For a long moment she looked up into his dark, attractive face, and she knew he could no more deny the compulsive desire that flared between them than she could. She reached for him then and drew his head down to hers, and kissed him. Her tongue seeking the magical depths of his sensuous mouth, her hands stroking and kneading his sleek bronzed skin. Discovering again the familiar strength and contours of his great body.

'Ah Helen, you have no idea how much I need this,' he groaned, trailing an exquisite line of kisses to her aching breasts. He closed his mouth around a rigid peaking nipple, suckling her hungrily.

Helen gave a gasping cry and arched into his mouth, her hands raking through his hair as he bestowed the same savage pleasure on the other. His tongue gently laved each straining nipple, his hands stroking, shaping the line of her waist, hip and thigh. Then he curved a strong arm round her to splay across her back, his mouth trailing lower, never ceasing the exquisite torment. His free hand reached to trace her lips, her throat, her breasts. Her legs parted eagerly, wanting, aching for him there. She felt the touch of his tongue in her navel and groaned her delight as his mouth dipped lower still and found those other lips and his skilful tongue teased the small, swelling bud of her passion.

'Please, Leon,' she cried out as her whole body shuddered in instant violent response. But still he continued until the pleasure was almost pain.

'Please,' she begged.

Leon heard her cry and lifted his dark head, feeling her hands rake up over his back, her teeth nipping his shoulder. He saw the blind hunger, the passion on her beautiful face, and with one powerful thrust plunged into her moist, tight, silken sheath and stayed. He wanted to make this last, but he could not. The sweet taste of her was on his tongue, the fiery heat of her consumed him, and for once his incredible control deserted him as her inner muscles clenched around him, drawing him on. And with a shuddering groan he thrust again and again, driving her, driving him, on a wild, primitive ride that exploded into a mutual orgasm that shattered anything he had experienced before.

Helen clung to Leon, her hands instinctively stroking his broad back as the trembling aftershock of their ferocious passion slowly faded away. The weight of his body pinned her to the bed, but it was a pleasurable weight and one she had missed the past week. She sighed languorously, her mind and body at last in accord.

Leon eased his weight off her and leant on one forearm looking intently down into her beautiful face.

'Finally defeated,' he stated huskily.

Her mellow mood shot to hell with two words, Helen shoved at his chest and he fell onto his back and she sat up. 'I was not defeated; I never asked you.'

It was her turn to stare down at him, breathless but infuriated by his arrogant assumption, the fact she had been going to ask him conveniently forgotten.

'You grabbed me,' she declared hotly and he had the nerve to laugh out loud.

'I meant I was admitting defeat, which you may not realise is an unheard-of occurrence for me.'

'Oh.'

Leon admitting defeat was too incredible for words. He was sprawled back on the bed with his hands behind his head. His black hair sexily tousled, a sensuous smile on his face. Anyone looking less defeated would be impossible to find, she thought wryly. He looked what he was: a supremely confident, sexually sated man.

'Though I suppose,' he drawled musingly, 'in the interest of married harmony we could call it a draw. I seem to recall you begging me not once, but twice.'

His dark eyes lit with laughter twinkled up at her and she could not help the laugh that bubbled out.

'You are impossible, and if we don't get dressed and downstairs our guests are going to come looking for us.'

'Okay.' He sat up and slid an arm around her shoulders. 'Are we okay now?'

Helen noticed he said 'we' and not 'you.' And for a moment she wondered if Leon really did care.

'If you have to think of an answer, forget it.'

'No, I mean, yes, we are fine,' she admitted blushing scarlet.

'Good.'

He gave her a brilliant smile and a swift, hard kiss on her mouth before leaping off the bed gloriously naked.

'Give me a couple of minutes and you can have the bathroom.' And she had the strongest feeling he was relieved by her answer.

'Hurry up, you lot,' Leon yelled from the foot of the steps of the aircraft. 'The holiday is over; get on board.'

'Is that any way to speak to our guests?' Helen demanded, walking up to him, Chris, Mary and the nanny bringing up the rear with the four lively children.

His dark eyes smiled wryly down at her as he snaked an arm around her and tucked her possessively against his broad shoulder. 'Probably not, but, much as I have enjoyed our holiday, I have discovered friends and family can seriously curtail one's sex life. The next time we go away we are going on the honeymoon we never had when we married.'

'That sounds promising,' Helen murmured, her heart singing as he bent his head and kissed her.

The last few days had been a revelation. Everyone had thoroughly enjoyed themselves; the days had been warm and fun with the children, the nights still cold in April, but hot for the adults in bed at night. Leon relaxed and loving was a sight to behold. Helen was almost sure it was love, though he had never said the words, but then neither had she.

'Yucky,' a little voice cried. 'I'm never going to kiss a girl.'

And the adults were all laughing as everyone boarded the aircraft.

'I have to get up,' Leon groaned.

'I rather thought you just had,' Helen returned wickedly, leaning up to rest her arms on his broad chest, her legs straddling his strong thighs.

'You, madam, are getting very risqué,' he chuckled, and in one deft movement Helen was on her back and Leon was looming over her. 'Not something I expected from the innocent I married.' His deep dark eyes smiled into hers. 'But then I never expected to…' And he stopped.

'To what?' Helen asked, lazily running her hands up over his broad chest.

'Nothing. I have to go.' He leapt off the bed, and paused

for a moment to stare down at her. 'There is something I have to tell you, but it can wait until tonight.'

'You sound serious.'

'I am about you.' Bending over, he brushed a tender kiss across her brow. 'Tonight.'

Spinning on his heel, he headed for the bathroom.

Helen hoarded his words like a treasure in her heart. She was sure he was going to tell her he loved her. Amazingly he had said he was serious about her, and after the last three weeks of what she could only describe as sheer bliss what else could it be?

Hopefully it would be the icing on the cake to a perfect day, Helen thought dreamily as she washed and dressed with care in a slim fitting natural linen skirt and matching short fitted jacket. On her feet she wore high heeled tan sandals and carried a matching purse. She was not taking Nicholas to school today, the nanny was, as Helen had an appointment at eleven.

At first when she had begun to feel tired and slightly nauseous she had put it down to the change in country, in food, and the much hotter weather in Greece than she was used to. It had been Mary who had pointed out that it could be something else. Helen hardly dared to hope, but she had made an appointment with Mary's gynaecologist for this morning.

She asked the driver to wait, and entered the private clinic.

Dr Savalas was a woman in her fifties with three children of her own, and immediately Helen felt at home with her, and told her the story of her accident and apologised in advance for probably wasting her time.

'So, let me get this straight, Mrs Aristides: you think you might be pregnant, but at the age of fourteen you had an accident. The doctor in Geneva told you the operation to repair your fractured pelvis was a success. Then added he was sorry but it was unlikely you would ever have a child. Have I got that right?'

Helen nodded her head.

'Well, give me his name, and let's see, shall we?'

An hour later Helen sat looking at Dr Savalas, her eyes swimming with tears of happiness. 'I really am pregnant?'

'Most definitely. I have checked with your doctor in Geneva and there is no real medical reason why you should not carry the child to full term. Though your pelvis has been weakened and you are quite small. To err on the side of caution, they suggest and I agree you should not attempt to have a natural birth, but opt for a Caesarean delivery.'

Helen floated out of the clinic on cloud nine, and climbed into the waiting car, a smile a mile wide on her face. When the driver asked her where to, without a second thought she said the bank. She had to tell someone or she would burst and Leon had the right to know first.

She skipped out of the car twenty yards from the bank, and told the driver to take a lunch break and she would call him later if she needed him. She felt like laughing out loud, but controlled the impulse, but could do nothing about the broad smile on her face.

CHAPTER TWELVE

'WELL, WELL, SOMEONE looks happy, and very pleased with themselves.'

Helen looked up in surprise at the handsome man who had stepped in front of her. 'Hello, Takis.'

'Let me guess, you're on your way to see Leon and the lawyers to collect the inheritance Delia left you.'

'No, with a bit of luck I am going to try and persuade Leon to take me out for lunch,' she said with a smile. After what Leon had told her she was wary of the man, but nothing could dent her euphoric mood today. Though she was slightly surprised by his comment. Why would Takis know anything about Delia's will? Not that it mattered. As far as she was concerned the inheritance was for Nicholas, full stop.

'You're a lucky lady and soon to be a very wealthy one. But nowhere near as lucky as Leon. He has control of everything and you as a beautiful bonus. I have got to hand it to him—he is brilliant and ruthless when it comes to business.'

There was something in his golden eyes that looked very like envy, and his less-than-flattering description of Leon dimmed her smile somewhat.

'I'm sorry, I have no idea what you are talking about,' she said slowly.

'Oh, come on, Helen, you may be blonde, but you're not an air-head. You must know that old man Aristides died before his daughter. Which meant Delia inherited forty per cent of her dad's fortune and according to my information she left eighty per cent of her estate to her son, and the rest to you. Surely you must have realised you and the boy stood to gain a heck of a lot more than if Delia had died first, much to Leon's dismay.'

Helen's smile vanished along with her sense of euphoria. 'What exactly are you trying to say?' she asked with a queasy feeling in the pit of her stomach.

'You don't know, you really don't know.' Taking her arm, he urged her towards a small pavement café. 'Join me for a coffee and I will explain.'

Over a cup of coffee Takis did just that.

'Leon and his father have always kept the majority of shares in Aristides International in the immediate family. They always had Delia's voting rights, though it might have been different if she had lived long enough to inherit the ones her mother had left her at twenty-five. But after the double tragedy and the discovery of Delia's will and her illegitimate child—you, Helen, became the wild card in the pack. As executor of the boy's estate Leon would not have had a problem, he could simply vote the child's shares the way he wanted to. But you could be a real problem for him.'

'This is all way over my head,' Helen muttered, taking a sip of her coffee with a growing feeling of dread.

'It is quite simple: you inherited twenty per cent of Delia's estate which includes eight per cent of the company shares from her father. I hold some, as do a host of other people whose family members have been involved in mergers in the past or simply bought them. The rest are held by big invest-ment companies that are more than satisfied with Leon's leadership. To give the devil his due he has a phenomenal business brain. But technically if we all joined together Leon would now no longer have a majority and your holding could be instrumental in voting him out of office.'

'I see.' Helen nodded.

'Don't get me wrong, Helen. You are a very beautiful woman, but you are in a very strong position, particularly as the child's guardian.'

'Leon is as well,' she cut in swiftly, and saw the look of pity in Takis' eyes.

'Are you sure about that? Check with your lawyer. I think you will find Leon is an executor of the boy's estate, not his guardian.' He shrugged his shoulders. 'It is not important. You're a lovely lady, and I hate to be the one to tell you but Leon had very compelling reasons to marry you, and not just for the boy. Your inheriting Aristides shares posed a threat— a very slight threat, it is true—to his absolute control of the bank. You must know what a control freak he is. So be careful.' And with that he up and left.

For a long time Helen simply sat and stared at the table with sightless eyes, Takis' revelation running though her brain, not wanting to believe the evidence before her. She recalled the appointment Leon had set up for her with Mr Smyth. He had congratulated her on her inheritance and on her forthcoming wedding and told her Leon was the executor of Nicholas' estate along with her and suggested he read the will in its entirety. But she had been in a hurry to go and buy her wedding dress, and refused his suggestion. She had told him she wanted to give the money to Nicholas. And then she recalled he had advised her to hold back on any decision until the will had passed probate. Had he been trying to warn her?

The adoption of Nicholas, which Leon had suggested and which had been instrumental in dissolving her resistance to him after only two days of marriage, suddenly took on a much more sinister light. If he was never the boy's guardian, as Takis had said, it made sense for Leon to press for adoption, then he would have exactly the same rights has her. How could any man be so ruthless, so Machiavellian?

'Would madam like anything else?'

Helen looked up at the waiter. 'No. No, thank you.' And he gave her the bill. A bitter smile curved her lips. Takis had left her to pay.

She walked through the streets of Athens her head bent and her mind in turmoil. When she finally reached the house it was after four. She heard the sound of childish laughter from the garden, and walked around the house to where the swimming pool was situated.

'Hi, Mum, watch me swim,' Nicholas yelled.

She watched him, blinking back the tears. Marta, the nanny was in the pool with him while Anna was sitting at the patio table with the driver, and both were keeping a watchful eye on the boy.

'Come on in,' Nicholas shouted.

'Not today,' she called back. 'I'm going upstairs to change.' And waving, walked indoors.

Not any day, she thought sadly, putting a protective hand on her still-flat stomach. Nicholas was Greek. Leon had been right about that. He was well looked after by people who adored him. He didn't really need her, she decided sadly. She didn't belong here, and she was going home.

She stopped halfway up the stairs, appalled at where her own selfish thoughts were leading her. Nicholas was her child as much as the child she carried in her womb, who would also be half Greek. She had no more right to deprive the child of its heritage than she had Nicholas. They would physically be cousins, and, in her heart, brothers.

She stripped off her clothes and flopped down on the bed and cried her eyes out. All her hopes and dreams shattered by a casual meeting and a few choice words from a man she barely knew.

A long time later she stood up and walked into the bathroom. She was mind numbingly frozen. She stepped into the shower and turned on the tap and let the hot water rush over her. But she felt as if she would never be warm again.

How could she have been such a blind fool? Such an idiot? she berated herself. She was still asking herself the same question when she sat before the dressing table in her bra and briefs to dry her hair.

'Hello, sweetheart.' Leon strode into their suite, a broad smile on his face. 'Wear something glamorous—I am taking you out to dinner.'

He wrapped an arm around her, pulling her gently up to her feet, his appreciative gaze sweeping over her scantily clad body, his eyes darkening as he would have pulled her close to kiss her. But Helen put her hands against his chest and pushed him away.

The veil of love had been torn from her eyes, and at last she was seeing him as he truly was. The ultimate tycoon. Tall and powerfully built, clad in a perfectly tailored pearl-grey suit. His hard, angular face and high cheekbones exuded an aura of ruthless power and absolute authority. How had she been so blind? she thought, seeing the flicker of impatience in his eyes. He hated to be thwarted in business or sex.

'I don't want to go out to dinner with you,' she said flatly. What should have been the most wonderful moment of her life was now a travesty. Scantily clad as she was, she wanted to get it over with and out of his sight as quickly as possible. 'I am pregnant.'

'You said you could not have children,' Leon declared harshly.

She stared at him. He didn't look delighted at the prospect. His face was more austere than she had ever seen it, his heavy lidded eyes were narrowed suspiciously on her, and a muscle flickered in his tanned cheek. Why was she surprised at his response? He had told her he didn't care about having a biological child; he probably did not want to split his wealth another way, she thought contemptuously.

'I was wrong; apparently a fractured pelvis does not preclude me getting pregnant after all, though it will prevent me from having a natural birth. The doctor told me I must have a Caesarean delivery.'

She could not believe she was talking to him so calmly when inside she was a seething mass of pain and fury. And she had been wrong about never feeling warm again; the few brief moments held against his long body had warmed her instantly, and she hated herself for it.

'Is it mine?'

That had to be the cruellest cut of all Helen thought savagely after a day that had seen her emotions go from dizzying happiness to absolute despair. She could not take any more.

'Leave me alone.' He disgusted her. 'Just leave me alone.'

She brushed past him. She had to get away.

'Sorry,' he said roughly, catching her by the arm and turning her back into the warmth of his body. 'Of course it is mine; I don't know what I was thinking of. Put it down to my natural cynical nature and forgive me.'

Held in his arms she could feel herself weakening. So what did it matter why he had married her? The irony of the situation suddenly hit her. In the beginning he had accused her of caring for Nicholas for money and the inheritance he had been sure she knew about, and had had the gall to call her the best paid nanny in the world. Yet all along it had been Leon who had been guarding his own incredible wealth.

'Helen, please, I really am sorry for doubting you for a minute. I would trust you with my life,' he said solemnly.

The shock of his repeated apology made her head spin. Too little, too late, she thought bitterly.

'Well, I sure as hell wouldn't trust you as far as I could throw you,' she lashed back. 'I met a friend of yours today and he was most informative. It seems the only reason you wanted Nicholas and I was to keep overall control of your bloody bank.'

His mouth hardened into a thin line as he demanded, 'What friend?'

'I bumped into Takis on the way to see you. Dr Savalas had confirmed my pregnancy and I wanted you to be the first to know. More fool me.' She glared at him. 'Takis stopped to congratulate me on becoming a wealthy woman and to warn me about you. We had a coffee together, and after chatting to him I suddenly found I had no desire to see you. Instead I decided to come back here.'

'Don't try my patience,' Leon said softly, his dark gaze roaming over her face and down to where her breasts were barely covered by the lace bra. 'What exactly did Takis say to you that changed the very willing wife I left in bed this morning into the tense angry woman before me now?'

She briefly closed her eyes against the pull of sensuality his blatant masculine look had aroused. The happiness of this morning felt like a lifetime ago now, Helen thought sadly.

'Takis told me the truth—something you seem to have an aversion to.' She shook her head, she hadn't the strength to yell at him and it took all her willpower to continue coolly, 'Ironic, isn't it, Leon? When you arrived at my home you accused me of being a gold-digger, when all the time it was you that was driven by money.'

She looked at him then and was slightly shocked by the

ferocious anger on his hard face, but not totally shocked. Like most powerful men he probably did not like to have his faults revealed.

'I know all about the wills,' she said flatly. 'The fact your father died first meant Delia inherited from his estate and consequently Nicholas and I got a lot more than you bargained for. Discovering we existed must have been one hell of a shock to you. No wonder you hotfooted it to England—your absolute control over Aristides International was threatened.'

She saw his face darken and thought he had a good right to look guilty. 'And your oh, so sensible offer of a convenient marriage while carefully avoiding telling me you were not named as Nicholas' guardian was a hell of a lot more devious than anything I ever did. As for adopting Nicholas, that was a master stroke.'

Helen stopped, unable to go on for a moment as the full extent of his deception struck her all over again. 'You were so efficient and considerate, even to arranging a meeting for me with Mr Smyth.'

She glanced up, her challenging gaze roaming over his hard face.

'Tell me, how much did you pay him?' she asked scathingly, recalling when he had asked her the same thing and flinging his own words back at him.

'That is enough,' he grated between clenched teeth. 'I never paid him a penny. And I never said I was Nicholas' guardian, I said I was a trustee of his estate.'

Thinking back she realised he was right, but it didn't alter the fact he had let her think it—his *muddy water* principle, no doubt.

'Maybe not.' She shrugged. 'He did tell me to read the will, but I was in a hurry to buy my wedding dress and didn't bother. How's that for a sick joke? But to give Mr Smyth his due he did tell me not to sign away my inheritance until I had thought about it for a few months. So he was honest, unlike you. Amazingly I was naive enough then to believe what you told me, but not any more.'

'If you shut up I can explain,' Leon began, lifting a hand towards her, and she knocked it away.

'Oh, please, spare your breath,' she said with a sarcastic lift of a finely arched brow. 'You tricked me into marriage. You tricked me into bed, and you would have quite happily let me trick myself out of the inheritance Delia left me.'

'No,' he growled and wrapping an arm around her waist, hauled her against him. 'That is not true and the main reason Takis has gone to such lengths to try to poison your mind against me is because I confronted him today with the final result of the investigation into Delia's drug taking. Takis is the party animal who handed out drugs like candy to his friends, Delia being one of them. The police can do nothing about it, because they can't prove it. But I told him if I ever saw him in Athens again I would destroy him.'

Helen believed him, but it didn't make any difference; it simply confirmed what a ruthless bastard Leon was. She drew in a deep, shuddering breath and suddenly she was intensely aware of his great body hard against her own. The scent of him, a mixture of tangy cologne and musky male, was clouding her senses and her cool control took a serious knock.

'You're probably right but it doesn't really matter any more,' she said flatly, determined not to be blinded by sex again. 'You don't need to worry; I have not changed my mind. I will still sign everything over to Nicholas. Now, if you don't mind, will you please leave?' Her head was suddenly spinning, her legs felt weak and she could not take any more.

'I want to get dressed,' she murmured, and felt herself falling against him.

* * *

Helen opened her eyes, and for a moment wondered where she was. She glanced around and realised she was lying on the bed. How did she get here? The door opened and Anna appeared with Nicholas by her side and a cup of tea in her hand. Helen pulled herself up to sitting position, wiping her damp hair from her face.

'What happened?' she asked.

'You fainted.' Anna smiled and stopped by the bed. 'Not unusual for a girl in your condition. Master Leon caught you and put you on the bed. He told me you were pregnant and now he is calling the doctor.' Handing her the cup, she added, 'Men are helpless at times like this. Now, drink that tea, and tell Nicholas you are fine.'

The little boy climbed on the bed.

As the events of the afternoon came back to her in all their horror, she hugged Nicholas close and with a few words and a cuddle she reassured him she was fine, and he was off like a shot to resume playing.

'Have you eaten today?' Anna questioned as he left. 'The chauffeur thought you were lunching with Master Leon, but he said you did not, and you are eating for two now, remember.'

'No, I'm afraid I missed lunch.' Helen shook her head and Anna left to return five minutes later with a ham salad, and left again.

After eating the salad Helen was about to get up and dress when the door opened again, and Leon walked in. He was the last person she wanted to see, she thought, her eyes flicking bitterly over him. He had lost the jacket and tie, his shirt was unbuttoned and if she had not known better she might have thought he was upset. A small grey haired man followed behind him, whom Leon introduced as the doctor.

'I don't need a doctor,' she began. 'I—'

'I will be the judge of that,' Leon said grimly, striding over to the bed and lowering her back down. 'You are too damn volatile to know what you need,' he muttered, pulling the sheet up over her thighs.

The doctor took her temperature, felt her pulse, asked a few questions, and nodded his approval when she mentioned Dr Savalas, while Leon stood in brooding silence listening to the whole proceedings.

'I will see the doctor out,' Leon declared, looking down at her with cold, hard eyes. 'Then I will be back.'

Helen inwardly shivered sensing the threat in his tone, and began to get up again. She needed to be dressed and on her feet to face him.

'Don't even think about getting up,' Leon commanded, and the doctor agreed. Helen silently fumed. Defying her autocratic husband's orders didn't bother her one bit, but the doctor was a different proposition. Nothing and no one, herself included was going to do anything to harm the precious life inside her.

Punching up the pillows, she eased her body up the bed. She had to stay in bed, but she didn't have to lie down. She had lain down enough for Leon Aristides, but not any more. Once she got out of this bed she was never sharing another bed with the man again.

For the sake of the child she carried and Nicholas she would stay and willingly sign everything over to the child or children. Leon was hard-headed and ruthless enough that once he got what he really wanted she knew he would leave her alone. It would not be a problem for him. He had told her himself his first marriage had been just such an arrangement for years; as for her, she could get used to anything in time. God knew, she had had enough practice, and this time she had the compensation of not one, but hopefully two children to love.

The door opened yet again and a glimmer of humour lightened her eyes. She was beginning to feel as if she were in the middle of Grand Central Station. But one look at the grim expression on Leon's hard face as he strode over to the bed and her amusement vanished. Suddenly she did not feel quite so brave, or so sure.

'The doctor said you must rest for a half an hour and then you can get up. Is there anything I can get you?'

'No.' She just wanted him to go. 'I think you have done quite enough for me already,' she drawled facetiously. 'I have nothing more to say to you except terms. If you wish to remain married, I am prepared to stay in this house for Nicholas' and our unborn child's sake, but not in this room. If you want a divorce I will give you one, but I keep the children.' At last she was taking back control of her life.

For a long tense moment there was silence. 'You really don't trust me at all. But this conversation is not over.'

His black eyes raked over her with insulting arrogance that did not help her budding confidence. 'We will discuss your terms later in my study after Nicholas is in bed. Don't make me have to come and fetch you.' He left, slamming the door.

Helen stood outside the study, reluctant to go in. Nicholas was safely tucked up in bed, and she had not seen Leon since he had stormed out of their room. She squared her slender shoulders, and nervously adjusted the neckline of the blue silk wrap around the top she had opted to wear. With not quite steady hands she smoothed the fabric of her slim fitting navy skirt down over her hips and drew in a deep steadying breath. She had to face Leon some time and she could no longer delay the confrontation.

The door opening interrupted her thoughts and Leon was standing in the aperture, a glass of what looked like whisky in his hand. He had changed, she noticed, into a crisp blue tailored shirt and dark blue trousers. They were a matching pair, the thought struck her. Not anymore, she amended swiftly, and lifted her head to fearlessly meet his gaze.

'Come in, we are expecting you,' he said smoothly, and stepped back to allow her to enter.

What did he mean 'we'? Helen was immediately thrown into confusion, her startled gaze sweeping around the room to rest on Chris Stefano standing by the desk.

'Chris. Hello,' she managed to get out through suddenly dry lips walking into the middle of the room. 'Nice to see you.'

'Take the social exchange as read,' Leon said curtly. 'Chris has some documents for you to sign and he is in a hurry.' And raising the glass to his mouth, he drained the contents.

Helen stopped, her slender body tensing. Chris was Leon's lawyer. Leon had said documents, plural. Had he already decided to take her up on her offer of, not just the inheritance, but a divorce as well? The sudden stab of pain in her heart made her wince.

'Are you sure you are all right?' Leon placed a hand on her arm.

She felt the pressure of his fingers against her bare skin and glanced up at him. His hard face looked drawn, his lips tight, and his deep set eyes had a troubled look about them. Concern for her? No, Leon was a man who had never truly cared for a woman in his life.

'Yes, I am fine.' She shrugged off his hand and walked to the desk. 'Show me where I have to sign.'

She forced herself to smile at Chris and picked up a pen from the desk.

'Sorry for the rush, Helen, but Mary and I are supposed to be going out to dinner. But you know your husband—if he wants something done, he wants it done yesterday.' He chuckled, and placed two papers in front of her. 'I am sure

Leon has explained everything to you, but if you want to read them go ahead.'

It took every bit of self control Helen possessed to smile back at Chris. 'No, that won't be necessary. But you could run the important points by me again.'

Was it a divorce Leon was going for? She cast a sidelong glance at her husband. He had moved to the opposite side of the room, where he was refilling his glass from a decanter. 'They are perfectly straightforward,' Chris said, and she quickly turned her attention back to him. 'The first is simply your acceptance of the money and shares, et cetera, Delia left you. I will need the name and number of the account you want them held in and the transfer will be through in five days.'

'Wait a minute! That's not right. I told Leon I want everything to go directly to Nicholas,' Helen exclaimed.

'I know, but he wouldn't hear of it. He told me before Easter to make sure everything was transferred into your name.'

'Before Easter, but...'

That could not be true, and yet she trusted Chris, and if it was true she had made the biggest mistake in her life today. She had believed everything Takis had told her, a man she hardly knew, and she had condemned Leon without giving him a chance to explain. She turned shocked eyes to Leon. He was leaning against the fireplace glass in hand, his expression inscrutable.

She thought back over the twelve weeks she had been married, and realised the preconceived notions she'd had of Leon had coloured her thinking the whole time. Being brutally honest, she knew it probably would not have mattered what he did. The wonderful lover, the great father, the magnificent diamonds he gave her, and most importantly his explanation of Louisa, while not pleasant to hear, had been truthful.

But still she had not credited him with an ounce of trust.

Instead she had believed a virtual stranger over him. What had she done?

'I am in a bit of a hurry, Helen,' Chris prompted. 'The other document is the first stage in adopting Nicholas.'

'No. I am not signing anything,' she stated, looking back at Chris. 'I thought…'

What she had thought was shaming and she stopped in mid-sentence.

'Like most women, my wife has trouble thinking clearly.' Leon addressed Chris as he crossed the room to Helen's side, closing his hands on her shoulders and turning her round to face him.

'I've told you before. Let me do the thinking.'

She was so heart-stoppingly beautiful both inside and out, and so thoroughly confused, and he knew he was to blame.

'You must sign the first document, Helen, to close the estate, afterwards you can do what you like with the money. As for the second document it can wait if you prefer. But Chris can't; he is in a hurry.' He held her shocked gaze, the air between them thickening with tension. He saw the kaleidoscope of emotions flickering in the violet depths of her eyes. Unlike him, she never could hide what she was feeling and he knew the moment she made her decision.

Helen signed both documents quietly.

'Why, Leon?' she asked quietly as Chris departed. 'Why did you not stop me this afternoon? Why did you ignore what I said about giving everything to Nicholas? I misjudged you so dreadfully. I didn't trust you an inch and I feel such a fool,' she admitted bleakly.

'No. I am the fool,' Leon declared, his dark gaze raking over her with a burning intensity that made her pulse race and her heart beat loudly in her breast. 'I ignored what you said, because I wanted you to have everything.'

'You said that once before,' Helen murmured. 'A couple of weeks after we married, when you took me to the bank.'

'I meant it then, and I mean it now,' he said simply, and, bending towards her, he had swept her up in his arms before she knew what was happening.

'What are you doing?' Helen cried inanely, flinging her arms around his neck.

'What I should have done weeks ago.'

He carried her to the sofa and, dropping down, he held her firmly on his lap. His dark gaze narrowed intently on her pale face.

'Told you I love you,' he said thickly.

Stunned, Helen stared at him like a woman transfixed.

'Me... You love me.' She had to be dreaming, or she had finally flipped and she was hearing voices.

'Yes, you, Helen. I never thought love existed until I met you.'

A great surge of hope swept through her. She wasn't crazy, Leon had said the words she had longed to hear.

'Oh, Leon, I—'

He lifted a finger and laid it against her soft lips.

'Say nothing. I have to do this now or I may never have the courage again.' He stopped her, a self deriding smile curving his mouth.

'From the day we met again in England I wanted you sexually. But you were right, and so was Takis in a way— my main motivation was to get you and Nicholas under my control. Technically I could have lost control of the company, but it would never happen. Some of the small shareholders like Chris and Alex and a few more would never vote against me. But I like to be thorough and when you offered to sign everything over to Nicholas, I said nothing and married you for my convenience, not yours,' he confessed in a rush.

Helen stirred restlessly on his lap, this was not what she

wanted to hear, but his arms gathered her closer. His dark eyes held hers, serious in their intent.

'I am trying to be honest, Helen—not pleasant, I know. I decided you were a clever, conniving woman, but on our wedding night I discovered in one way at least you were completely innocent. I was amazed and delighted, and in my arrogance I told myself I had a willing, sexy woman in my bed and an heir to inherit after me. What more could a man want?'

'That is so chauvinistic.' Helen shook her head. But she wasn't surprised. Leon was never going to be the new age man women's magazines raved about.

'I know, and I am ashamed to say I carried on thinking that way for quite a while. I told myself the incredible urge to make love to you every time I looked at you was just sex, I couldn't admit it was more.'

'And was it more?' she asked, willing him to say he loved her again, because she still could not quite believe him.

Leon smiled and buried his lips in the silken scent of her hair for a moment.

'Oh, I think you always knew it was more,' he husked, his dark gaze returning to her upturned face. 'It was more the first time I had to leave you to go to New York and I bought you a ring. It was more every time I held you in my arms and made love to you. It was more when I told Chris to make sure you inherited everything you were entitled to. I loved you but I was too much of a coward to tell you.'

There was no doubting the sincerity in his dark eyes, and she ran a gentle finger down the side of his face, her heart swelling in her breast. He caught her hand in his and raised it to his lips and she was powerless against the softness of his small caress and the flood of emotions it evoked. She stirred restlessly on his lap and was aware of the hard strength of his aroused body beneath her. And wriggled again.

'Don't do that.' Leon tightened his grip on her hand. 'Let me finish. I finally admitted to myself I loved you the night of the party. I stood with you in my arms and knew you were my world. I thanked you for marrying me and I had never felt such happiness in my life. Then like Nemesis, Louisa arrived.'

'She does not matter.' Helen lifted her other hand to curl around the nape of his neck and brought his face towards hers. She finally believed Leon loved her; this big, beautiful, austere man loved her.

'All that matters is that you love me, and I love you,' she said unsteadily, her eyes swimming with tears of joy.

'Helen,' he husked, 'I don't deserve you but, God help me, I will never let you go.'

He kissed her with a reverence, a deep tender passion that touched her very soul.

'You love me.' He lifted his head to look deep into her eyes, a gleam of uncertainty in his own.

'You really love me?' he asked in a voice that was raw with feeling. 'Can you can forgive my less than honourable intentions in the beginning?'

'I truly, passionately love you,' she said adamantly. She did not like to see her proud, arrogant husband looking humble. Well, maybe just this once, she thought, happiness bubbling inside her. 'And I will forgive you anything because I love you.'

So much had happened in the past three months. So many misunderstandings and misconceptions, mostly held by her, and on a more serious note she added hesitantly, 'But can you forgive me?' The past could not be changed, but to go forward she knew she had to face and resolve her own demons. 'I think I knew I loved you from the day we married. I admitted as much to myself when you came back from New York the last time. But I never trusted you as I should. I believed the worst over Louisa, and I believed Takis instead of listening to you.'

'So long as you listen to me in future I don't give a damn,' he stated fiercely, and she laughed out loud. Her arrogant, powerful husband was back. 'As I said before I would trust you with my life. Which reminds me—' he speared a hand through her hair, a solemn expression on his darkly attractive face '—are you sure that this pregnancy is safe and what you want? I don't want you put at the slightest risk. I can live without a biological child, but I can't live without you.'

His sentiment was heart-warming but his unspoken suggestion of a termination horrifying. 'Don't be ridiculous. Of course I want our child, and I will be fine, and so will the baby. You're probably worrying because you lost your first child.'

'Actually this will be my first child. After years of marriage when nothing happened Tina said she was fine, so I thought I could not have children, and by that time the marriage was basically a sham anyway. I finally decided to seek a divorce, thinking Tina would leap at the chance to have a family with someone else, but I was wrong. I had not slept with her in over a year when she turned up in Greece for Christmas and crawled into my bed. I am ashamed to say I was quite drunk at the time, and later when she said she was pregnant I could do nothing about it.' He shrugged a shoulder.

'The car accident that killed her was in New York in June, the baby the doctor delivered was full term, so could not possibly have been mine.' An ironic smile twisted his firm mouth. 'The baby survived for a few hours and bore a striking resemblance to her African-American fitness instructor who died with her.'

Helen was speechless. It was the same ironic smile he had given her when she had told him she was sterile, and now she knew why. This strong, proud man had suffered the same pain as her. She placed a tender hand either side of his head and kissed him with all the love and compassion in her heart.

'Ah, Helen.'

Leon groaned and deepened the kiss as passion took over, and within moments Helen was beneath him on the sofa. His hand swept over her breast and thigh to the hem of her skirt, and he froze.

'You're pregnant; is it allowed?'

'Well, some of your more erotic positions might not be viable after a while, but right now anything goes.'

Later that night in bed, with all barriers down and the freedom to reveal their deepest emotions, they made love with soft words, subtle caresses and a tenderness and passion and hunger that superseded everything that had gone before until finally they fell into an exhausted sleep wrapped in each others arms.

Seven months later Leon, all gowned up, walked beside the gurney, holding Helen's hand as they wheeled her towards the operating theatre.

She looked so small even with their child in her body and he had never been so terrified in his life. He loved her so much with a depth of passion that seared his soul. The last few months had been the happiest he had ever known. She was his life, his soul mate, his reason for living, and if anything happened to her his life would be over. But he let none of his fear show as he gently touched her soft cheek.

'Don't worry, I am here.' She looked at him with wide trusting eyes and her beauty tore at his heart. For a man who had never known emotions until she came into his life, Leon's suddenly threatened to get the better of him and he had to blink away the moisture in his eyes.

'I love you and I am going to stay with you every step of the way. Hold onto me and you will be fine.' She gave him a beautiful smile and squeezed his hand as they entered the theatre.

* * *

'Congratulations, Helen, Leon, you have a perfect little baby girl.'

Helen's violet eyes blazing with joy roamed delightedly over the baby. 'A girl. A daughter.' She smiled and glanced up at a hovering Leon. 'Our daughter.'

'I can't believe it,' Leon declared, his dark eyes luminous with tears of happiness and love as they moved from the tiny baby to his wife. 'She is beautiful, just like you—thank you, my love,' he husked, and bent his head to place a soft kiss against her lips. 'I swear I will love and protect you and Nicholas and our miraculous little girl with the last breath in my body.'

Helen saw a tear slide down the sharp blade of his cheekbone. She grasped his hand in hers, her lips parting in a slow, beatific smile. 'I know you will, Leon. I love and trust you totally and I thought we might call our daughter Delia. What do you think?'

'Delia… Yes, of course, I think it is perfect,' Leon agreed, his heart overflowing with love for this tiny, tough, compassionate woman, his wife. 'Delia brought us together and gave us our son, Nicholas. It is fitting.'

'Then you better go and find Nicholas,' Helen murmured drowsily. 'So he can meet his sister.'

Leon did not go immediately; he waited until the doctor was finished, and stayed by her side until she fell into an exhausted sleep. Then he bent to kiss her lips once more, and smooth some silken strands of hair from her brow.

'Sleep well, my love, and when you awake Nicholas and baby Delia and I will be by your side, I promise. Now and for ever more,' he vowed, his voice thick with emotion and pride. Only then did he straighten up, and leave to fetch Nicholas. A man with a dazzling, determined gleam in his dark eyes. A man on a mission for life.

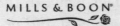

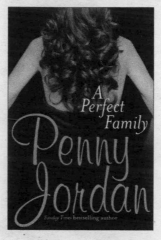

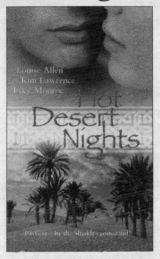

FREE

4 BOOKS AND A SURPRISE GIFT!

We would like to take this opportunity to thank you for reading this Mills & Boon® book by offering you the chance to take FOUR more specially selected titles from the Modern Romance™ series absolutely FREE! We're also making this offer to introduce you to the benefits of the Mills & Boon® Reader Service™—

- ★ **FREE home delivery**
- ★ **FREE gifts and competitions**
- ★ **FREE monthly Newsletter**
- ★ **Books available before they're in the shops**
- ★ **Exclusive Reader Service offers**

Accepting these FREE books and gift places you under no obligation to buy; you may cancel at any time, even after receiving your free shipment. Simply complete your details below and return the entire page to the address below. You don't even need a stamp!

YES! Please send me 4 free Modern Romance books and a surprise gift. I understand that unless you hear from me, I will receive 6 superb new titles every month for just £2.89 each, postage and packing free. I am under no obligation to purchase any books and may cancel my subscription at any time. The free books and gift will be mine to keep in any case.

P7ZEE

Ms/Mrs/Miss/Mr...Initials ....
BLOCK CAPITALS PLEASE
Surname ....
Address ....

....

....Postcode ....

Send this whole page to:
The Reader Service, FREEPOST CN81, Croydon, CR9 3WZ

Offer valid in UK only and is not available to current Mills & Boon® Reader Service™subscribers to this series.
Overseas and Eire please write for details. We reserve the right to refuse an application and applicants must be aged 18 years or over. Only one application per household. Terms and prices subject to change without notice. Offer expires 31st July 2007. As a result of this application, you may receive offers from Harlequin Mills & Boon and other carefully selected companies. If you would prefer not to share in this opportunity please write to The Data Manager at PO Box 676, Richmond, TW9 1WU.

Mills & Boon® is a registered trademark owned by Harlequin Mills & Boon Limited.
Modern Romance™ is being used as a trademark. The Mills & Boon® Reader Service™ is being used as a trademark.